Avoiding
Spiritual
Mediocrity

Time for the Church to Get Back Its Savor Among Humanity, and Its Favor Among the Annals of an All-Mighty God.

BOB ALLEN

ACKNOWLEDGMENTS

All scripture quotations unless otherwise marked are taken from the King James Version of the Bible.

Scripture quotations marked AMP are "Scripture quotations taken from the Amplified® Bible, Copyright © 1954, 1958, 1962, 1964, 1965, 1987 by The Lockman Foundation and Used by permission." (www.Lockman.org)

Scripture quotations marked GW are Scriptures from GOD'S WORD®, © 1995 God's Word to the Nations. Used by permission of Baker Publishing Group.

All Scripture quotations marked NKJV are Scriptures from the New King James Version®. Copyright © 1982 by Thomas Nelson, Inc. Used by permission. All rights reserved.

Scriptures marked MSG are "Scriptures taken from *The Message*. Copyright © 1993, 1994, 1995, 1996, 2000, 2001, 2002. Used by permission of NavPress Publishing Group."

Scripture quotations marked Darby are taken from the Darby Translation of the Bible.

Scripture quotations marked ASV are taken from the American Standard Version of the Bible.

Scripture marked ISV are taken from the Holy Bible: International Standard Version®. Copyright © 1996-forever by The ISV Foundation. ALL RIGHTS RESERVED INTERNATIONALLY. Used by permission.

Scripture quotations marked TPT are from The Passion Translation®. Copyright © 2017, 2018 by Passion & Fire Ministries, Inc. Used by permission. All rights reserved. ThePassionTranslation.com.

CONTENTS

INTRODUCTION

The Church while it has always had individuals within its ranks who struggle with spiritual mediocrity, the amount of those in the today realm of churches is multiplying faster than a den of rabbits. I see this in the way many easily accept the addition of worldly things into the work of ministry and fellowship today. This combining of a Godly era of truths to the world's deceit and evils creates confusion in the hearts and minds of those who call Christ, Lord.

Though nothing in scripture details a purpose for mediocrity it does serve the enemy's purpose of ignorance and immaturity being among believers, so their spiritual status is uncharacteristic of the Father, Son, and Holy Spirit. Pulpits who nurture congregants by this new age of blending scriptural truths with worldly precepts and calling it the gospel of Christ, are in God's sight as disdained and immature of the work of the Spirit of God. As it is not in the annals of scripture for those who impart the word to God's children to demean its purpose or undermine its authority for the sake of self or worldly endowment, both are characteristic of evil.

Shining light upon issues taboo among churches, requires both a revealing of any ill-mannered doctrines afoot and any narrated text homiletically structured for divisive purposes. Thus, in the aspects of revealing such things I call your attention to the fact two thirds of scripture are written for revealing the one we call Satan, the Devil, and the forces of darkness that prevail.

Jesus himself mentions the Devil more than He mentions the Holy Spirit. All of it is to reveal believers are to have knowledge of his manner of evils and wickedness used against them. Since the world at large has no understanding of the enemy's ways and many of his deceits, lies accepted by the world have entered churches and are being incorporated into doctrines in these later days.

So, things revealed relevant to you knowing and understanding what paramount is to any believer's spirit life, is vital to you having strong faith and a perception of who you are in the sight of God.

Nothing in the pages of this book is said for the purpose of me creating guilt, or despair, or worry over what one is doing in a life with Christ. Nor is it to create conflict or anger over what has taken place within the churches of Christ body. It is all to shine light upon issues that today promote spiritual mediocrity and how much of it can be seen in the Church's past giving believers an opportunity to seek forgiveness amid a world without repentance.

The most frequent question I get asked, is why make all or any of this known can we not just love others for Christ? To them I say your new life that comes with servitude to the Father in revealing Christ must be one removed from past positions of sin to rightfully uphold a position in His kingdom. Since humanity along with the Church's past is filled with mistakes extremely grievous to God and under toll of judgment, many though done out of ignorance and an immaturity, are not being avoided by today's leaders.

Clearly God does reveal evils along with the good but the intent and concern in His heart is we take heed to truths about it and do only as He instruct within the annals of scripture. Avoiding spiritual mediocrity is something every believer must do, but any knowledge of how it occurs and one's authority to prevent it can be challenging if an imposed ignorance and/or immaturity is present.

Many statements I make within, are not for a manner of ridicule though that is how much of it will be seen. But I believe revelation to what has occurred by denominations, religious organizations, pulpits, and ministries needs to be known. As it will reveal that the mistakes for the sake of control done by past leadership is filtering back into a current day ministry that today prevents many from knowing who they are as a born-again child of God.

Thus, believers must learn how to avoid anything that says they are less than what God says they are to be. This is so faith required to fulfill such a destiny is not defaulted or denied by a mediocre state of spiritual knowing.

You will see I mention righteousness a lot in this book, and the reason is believers today are not living out a right standing in Christ revealing a mediocrity is afoot among the annuls of what scripture says about Christian living. That day of great harvests is here, and Christ Church participants are to be of a spiritual maturity enabling them to fulfill a part in a plan laid out millennia ago. But way too many are busily indulging in the ways of the world, making it time the Church gets back its savor among humanity, and its favor among the annuls of an All-Mighty God.

CHAPTER ONE
Deceptions

This aspect of mediocrity present within the Church is not new, however among all the anxiety and ambitiousness of today we see many believers have a certain level of it appearing. And it is creating an unresponsive attitude toward spiritual issues relevant to a God outcome for His children. Many pulpits believe it is not necessary to reveal those things that have plagued the Church during its 2000-year existence. But I on the other hand am led to do otherwise, and believe it is time for a revealing of truth to show there is disparity over God's plan present in the will of humanity.

For believers to see how an enemy continues to deceive many to the degree they see themselves rightfully endowed to fulfill a will completely contrary to one born out of God, reveals the plans of God focused upon His creation are today not as He says. Thus, we now have a Church filled with those who are incapable of exerting any dominion, power, and authority as offspring of an All-Mighty God, because of ignorance of the facts. Truth of all a believer must know about spiritual mediocrity has somehow gotten covered over or is at worst purposely being left out of learning by pulpits that nurture God's offspring.

Today a large portion of Christ body sees no evil in much of the manners afoot, evident they are without knowledge of who they truly are in the sight of God. Seeing oneself not as God sees you, is an age-old deception of the devil and something he has done ever since the fall of Adam. Any idea of creation freely flowing through the social spectrum of humanity flawed to the degree it promotes not only a hate of self but of others, is a direct work of evil through ignorance driven by his devilish intent.

The world is deceptively mannered toward evil therefore its behavior reveals an image to be flaunted evident in the fact human nature is carnally sinful. But the Church however views today's worldly activity by doctrinal ideals showing it is something to be embraced and not relevant to one's spiritual maturity.

Teachings tenured in churches today carry a narrow-minded view of man and woman for the sake of rendering connection to any social issue effecting one's overall wellbeing. It is not by mistake since in the annals of scripture the ways of how to nurture Christ siblings into spiritual maturity still reveals His image.

Gen 1:27 *So* *God created man in His own image, in the image and likeness of God He created him; male and female He created them.*

Deceiving Humanity

God has a way of revealing to His children what is going on and how the truth in scripture helps make spiritual sense of what needs to be done regardless of churches who allow evils to distort its true purpose. Life regarding experiences out of character to God is an area often void of any truth by pulpits who are gleaning scripture for the daily deliverance. One reason mediocrity abides in the light of such truths in the Church is that open works of the Spirit of God are missing from congregations.

Thus, they are ending up with believers who accommodate a worldly mannerism into a faith that is to be without a surrender to societal trends. For believers to be conscious of truths regarding this issue we need to look at several things both past and present but let us begin with what some in the world of today say about humanity, and its time of extinction.

An ideology born out of an evil intent, is taking advantage of people's ignorance promoting hatred and having no concern for life and its purpose on earth. And if you were to add the deceptive cry for our destruction to preserve the world presented in this hour by emotionally and senselessly driven individuals. Proof they are of another spirit and are a present danger when you consider how these deceptive individuals keep maneuvering into positions of society, to control you having a right to live in it.

Today many believers allow themselves to be driven along by a hate filled doldrum and find faith hard to exercise as they accept a new worldly presentation of it. This obviously creates large portions of the Church fulfilling a part in a plan they know nothing about and those defiant of a salvation process God determined to be successful in says they will be spending eternity with the devil.

The fact there are many believers who are convinced within the evolution of all things are certain spiritual attributes, that based on an ideology of cohabitation of species, coerces all to willingly adapt to many social ills. Reveals people are deceived and think those who tell such lies are smarter than God and believe they are the perfect humans.

The similarity between the world and the Church is seen in the fact that just like the religious leaders in Christ day of whom He said made disciples who were twice the devil they were. Is being done today by deceptive illusions of salvation through acceptance of sin, a senseless ideal that even the religious bunch knows not to accept.

Math 23:15 [15] *Woe unto you, scribes and Pharisees, hypocrites! for ye compass sea and land <u>to make one proselyte</u>, and when he is made, <u>ye make him twofold more the child of hell than yourselves</u>.*

Pulpits today patronize a present culture that is deceived by its own vanity and entitlement, and fulfill peer expectations as a new era of ministerial dynamics and over-the-top performance arrives.

These same pulpits ignore any true spiritual nurturing God has expectation of occurring among His children as they mix an evil worded acceptance of life issues into preambles of spiritual truth. These are individuals who see themselves smarter than God and believe they are right in what they do.

Another area having strong influence on believers is society's senseless ideology affecting sexual positions on earth by activist and women we call feminist, who support the evil in thinking males are chauvinistically biased toward females. This one ideology has been evilly introduced into society to create generations of men who see themselves unworthy to be viewed as partners of an opposite sex.

As, they will no longer see themselves a factor in influencing society by a male genderism they believe they are as society says, without intellect or mental equality. And though none of this is true, for the feminist and their supporters it is all about deception by self-induced fascisms.

Today's society influencers refuse to accept there is a higher power at work here in that both sexes are here to *complement* each other's God created purpose, not to conflict over any sexual oddities someone might conceive by lies from a deceptive devil.

If we add the fact that neither created themselves, it gives way to a discerning each is holding an accountability that in the day of judgement will be given up to the one who created both. And any ill viewed presentations of sexism are to be seen as carnal expectations.

The real issue becomes, this kind of deceiving social activism affects society in such a way that a self-imposed hate appears and destruction of any perception of marriage, sex, or how society views both males and females occur. And it is all grounded in an evil intent that defies fundamental truths of procreation, but is set in place to promote unions of those who would allow themselves to be liberal sexual oddities of today's defined social normality.

The difficulty in cleaning up these uncharacteristic manners of believers in the churches of today is they openly think everything is to be intertwined into the gospel. And is deceptively planted to such a degree it is getting hard to discern issues of truth God reveals.

Believers must know it is the devil who plots to disrupt their presence on this earth seen in the fact today's secular humanist are promoting there are other ways for compatible unions of males and females based on foundations of Godly principles. Thus, a very large portion of the body of Christ now accepts this evil ideology that flies in the face of scriptural truths that reveal otherwise.

These issues are a direct result of spiritual mediocrity that has been purposely set forth by an activist's society and pulpits who are more fearful of a rebuke than the God who created them. Liberates for centuries have used sexual perversity to deceive the freedom of choice to be married promoting lifestyles different from any God would be a partner in and made many see marriage as essentially flawed in the sight of human liberal morals.

They have also made churches neutral on the matter and more interested in staying in tune to the latest humanist social trend. There are pulpits who may not openly promote liberal ideologies but are replacing biblical teachings on proper sexual behavior with biased humanist ideals. This is happening because churches are filled with secularly based people willing to be neutered, in a spiritual sense, by liberal idealisms rather than scriptural truths.

Deceptions

In today's societal platforms this kind of activity enforces many pulpits to wholly expect congregants to accept annals of deceit put forth about bias liberal ideals and its evil proponents. Even though much of it aligns to creating spiritual ignorance while promoting a societal acceptance of unity of males with males, and females with females, and a senselessness over gender equality.

So, how did we get to a point in our churches and society where we hate each other's sexual presence and willing to demise the very value each brings into the creation? Part of the answer is laid out in our past, in a time when there was no bible or written scriptures to reflect on for guidance or edification of one's *soul*.

It is revealed to us in the stories we now read of how an enemy came and deceived a humanity created in our present sexes' forms of males and females. In them are enlightened truths for knowledge and understanding of what is taking place today that also took place in the beginning.

Believers unable to deal spiritually with homosexuality or this new gender diversity by considering truths from God's word shows how far they have fallen toward this worldly biased knowledge of things. Thus, by any amount of Godly sense why are they no longer able to evaluate these as actions unacceptable to God for humanity, and the Church?

This kind of devalued thinking is constantly being put forth to destroy not just morals and ethics, but any Godly values to be taught and learned by His creation. One reason sexual perversity is at the forefront in many areas of our society is, it is being enforced by an enemy committed to killing, stealing, and destroying the truth. All to make one's life a state of mediocrity before a God who expects otherwise from those He has delivered from such senselessness. And those who satisfy their evil nature by acting out carnal episodes of intolerance, despair, disobedience, are promoting deceptions of life.

Today's churches continue to declare it is a sin to live a lifestyle against God, but many of these same churches rarely change the lives of those congregating within them. As too many new believers are struggling with tenants of faith, and are often seen as unwilling to change. Any inability to do what is right in the sight of God helps the enemy's efforts and emboldens what scripture says concerning, all have sinned and fallen short of His glory.

Rom 3:23 *Because all have sinned, and come short of the glory of God;*

The fact much of this is seen by Him as sinful, does not seem to be a factor in a process of hermeneutically rendering instructions for congregations that lends to an acceptance of liberal doxology.

There was one man who had an exclusive position regarding sin, Jesus Christ the Son of God who came into this world without sin and took all of it upon himself at the cross. He alone proclaims our freedom from it so everyone can be free from sins ability to kill their created purpose and remove them from God's eternal plan. And the truth that makes this known comes only by the Spirit and the word of God.

John 3:16 *For God so loved the world, that he gave his only begotten Son, that whosoever believeth in him should not perish, but have everlasting life.*

Believers need to ask themselves, why are worldly manners of sin having a greater influence in the Church today after some 2000 years of existence? It is all about deceptions of a spiritual kind through liberal doxology narrated for a purpose of control. Socialist ideas undergird most of our civil disruption and hatred in our social tenure today. Thus, it is not a mistake it is here by a perpetual evil deception that has forever been an obstacle to humanity and its true existence on earth.

We can see this in the current events of a pandemic that is being deceptively tenured to power and authority by those who see it as an opportunity to invoke egos thriving on public ignorance and fear.

In a time when progressivism thrives God is presently in an era of grace towards us, but still judges. And since these deceivers are out of character to the culture of His kingdom, they just like all of creation will be accountable to Him for how they lived for purposes of compliance to senseless ideals, of which there is no escape.

Rev 20:12-13 [12] *And I saw the dead, small and great, stand before God; and the books were opened: and another book was opened, which is the book of life: and the dead were judged out of those things which were written in the books, according to their works.* [13] *And the sea gave up the dead which were in it; and death and hell delivered up the dead which were in them: and they were judged every man according to their works.*

Learning How Iniquity Works

It is important believers understand the character of sin by using basic spiritual sense you see from scriptures that reveal every state of perverted behavior to appear before God is grievous to Him no matter the works of sin presented in it.

Rom 1:20-32 (MSG) *By taking a long and thoughtful look at what God has created, people have always been able to see what their eyes as such can't see: eternal power, for instance, and the mystery of his divine being. So nobody has a good excuse.*

Anyone who denies there is a God after seeing what was created by a Divine power are conformed to the effects of wickedness and evils removing them from an eternal purpose. All by a behavior of sin that eventually cost both present and eternal life, anyone abiding in such a state are without an acceptable excuse.

21 What happened was this: People knew God perfectly well, but when they didn't treat him like God, refusing to worship him, they trivialized themselves into silliness and confusion so that there was neither sense nor direction left in their lives. 22 They pretended to know it all, but were illiterate regarding life.

Truth regarding sin's attempt to satisfy a carnal nature destroys the working of it, however, sin apparent in the fact it is still among us is a testimony every individual can still choose to do. But it will degrade their consciousness of a creator and bring a form of self-idolism that ends up trading a created glory for a darkness of evils and immoral deception.

23 They traded the glory of God who holds the whole world in his hands for cheap figurines you can buy at any roadside stand. 24 So God said, in effect, "If that's what you want, that's what you get." It wasn't long before they were living in a pigpen, smeared with filth, filthy inside and out.

Thus, immorality becomes a lifestyle or a natural way of living as it constantly satisfies a nature to live life filled with perversity. This results in an internal conflict of *soul* and *spirit* that erringly deems any Godly living is conflicting and without content as they encourage others to live the same lifestyle.

Thus, to freely accept all manners of lust and sinful activity through sexual perversity normalizes any morals and equity of life.

25 And all this because they traded the true God for a fake god, and worshiped the god they made instead of the God who made them—the God we bless, the God who blesses us. Oh, yes!

We can see how they garner this perverse mindset thinking they are above God and that what they choose to do in this lifestyle of fleshly darkness is far better than anything God will do for them.

[26] Worse followed. Refusing to know God, they soon didn't know how to be human either women didn't know how to be women, men didn't know how to be men. [27] Sexually confused, they abused and defiled one another, women with women, men with men all lust, no love. And then they paid for it, oh, how they paid for it emptied of God and love, godless and loveless wretches.

There is an end to all of this? Individuals' unconscious of their created purpose forced to seek out and fulfill sinful acts by a carnal love of self are void of a love for God, end up paying a vital price.

[28] Since they didn't bother to acknowledge God, God quit bothering them and let them run loose.

God has never done anything against a person's will, they are free to choose to do whatever they want, that includes choosing to deny Christ and the God who created them. They are in constant warfare of mind and heart trying to reason out and justify events in their life. Inventing new evils and wicked plots to try and satisfy a lust from torment, deception, lies, and spiritual miss truths.

[29] And then all hell broke loose; rampant evil, grabbing and grasping, vicious backstabbing. They made life hell on earth with their envy, wanton killing, bickering, and cheating. Look at them: mean-spirited, venomous, [30] fork-tongued God-bashers. Bullies, swaggerers, insufferable windbags! They keep inventing new ways of wrecking lives. They ditch their parents when they get in the way. [31] Stupid, slimy, cruel, cold-blooded.

Such ideals are designed to provoke others to engage in sinful lifestyles claiming anyone against such living are just bigots, social intolerants, phobist, racist, or self-righteous white supremacist. And yet all of this is to cover up a desire for immorality that is completely defiant of God and what He does, because it defies selfishness, a deceptive factor the devil takes advantage of.

[32] And it's not as if they don't know better. They know perfectly well they're spitting in God's face. And they don't care, they hand out prizes to those who do the worst things best!

Current ideologies like liberal progressivism promotes sins and evils by disrupting society through social narratives that have today created a secular activism that has even invaded churches. This is revealed in the social pandering to bring others into congregations not by a ministry of truth but by emotionally charged expletives, that say your sin can easily be narrated to appear as just an incorrect perception of you.

While liberalism is nothing more than an ideological choice the fact is it exists and continues to apply its socialist's ideology to platforms in society's educational, governmental, political, and even religious environments all to promote unrest meant to cover up any spirit of deception within its agenda.

Those ministries and pulpits helping to engineer society to be void of moral and ethical standards should be charged with being out of character to God by a politically correct phobia.

Deceiving The Church

We have seen how the enemy is using society and those who adhere to liberal pretext to promote deceptions among us but to learn more about why believers are becoming mediocre we need to move from this order of idealisms and look at the history of the Church.

In the early years of the Church age around $2^{nd,}$ and 3rd century AD, pious leadership saw fit to remove all of Israel's influence and replace any literal knowing of scripture with platonic teachings that have formed most of today's religious doctrines. This was an act of deception to position the church into a caustic denial of spiritual exhortation which was instrumental in forming a distrust of Israel that unfortunately carries through to modern times.

The fact that Israel is still God's chosen nation, did not affect the bringing in of teachings such as replacement theology that has removed any ordained love for her. As many in the church are anti-Israel because of this and other teachings, she no longer has right to be the Church as a part of God's glorious kingdom.

Clearly there is a deceit of truth in scriptural doctrine God has laid out to us, as He says we are all founded upon Israel's history. A nation He intends to save at the end of all of this, as God underlines in His word the fact, He has an eternal plan in mind that includes Jew and Gentile to be as He states, *His Spiritual Offspring*.

Gal 3:28 [28] *There is neither Jew nor Greek, there is neither bond nor free, there is neither male nor female: for ye are all one in Christ Jesus.*

It is humanity that is ordained to bring about a spiritual lineage out of its presence on this earth and any characteristic of Him is not to be in any aspect under an influence of the devil. The process to distort God's purpose and bring about evil and wicked works is as seen in the present idea of societal church deceits.

Today we have churches accepting this present mindedness of genderism and in agreement to the latest homosexual norms as is previously mentioned. All based upon an evil deception that says gender is not defined by one's sexual physiology at birth but rather by psychological pretext and therefore subject to an influence saying inclusivity is for an equity of life.

Math 19:4-6 *And he answered and said unto them, Have ye not read, that he which made them at the beginning made them male and female,*

Any believer knowing the truths from scripture would perceive this senselessness as a realm of psychosis layered with ideal sexist's perversity activated in the thinking of persons who are void of truth.

Sexual perversity is a common work of the enemy revealed all throughout scripture. Today we have societal deceits being put forth to affect our social unity and the church as we have media programs and television shows all trying to reveal a sexual influence, by role modeling males and females as power wielding socialites.

Every liberal media outlet promotes inclusivity and sexuality in almost every genre format. Thus, attempting to narrate acceptance of sin and evils by implying there is nothing unique about males or females, both are in an equal dimension sexually. However, males and females virtually have nothing to do with what they are sexually, so to think anyone can change or control it reveals an evil manner is afoot.

Written in the scriptures are story after story of relationships of both males and females showing us each impact historical aspects of all creation. But our enemy the devil is busily at work placing into believers' minds thoughts that take away any truth of God's creative work in them according to their sex. Therefore, it is very important all believers discern things correctly so they will not be detrimental to health and wellbeing, and end up deceived.

Heb 5:14 *(NKJV) But solid food belongs to those who are of full age, that is, <u>those who by reason of use have their senses exercised to discern both good and evil</u>.*

The reason why truth from God's word is so imperative for your spiritual maturity, is it trains you to have an ability to discern what is good and what is evil around you. Believers garnering spiritual mediocrity become ill-minded toward God's purpose of things, even of what a male and female are in context to sex in the creation, and find themselves void of any truth when it comes to security of *soul*. And often fault others for their situation because they desperately attempt to remove any stigma that says they are not as God says.

This is a clear warning that amongst us are workers of iniquity willing to defy their own presence of being, and yours as well. The thing that comes to mind, is for the Church warfare against evils influencing humanity's sexual diversity is missing, and reveals a willingness to accept narratives the gospel is not aligned to for a transforming of *soul*.

The fact churches no longer see certain scripture essential to the work of ministry creates a platform for ignorance to prevail, thus voids in the knowing necessary to fully mature leaves its occupants in a state of immaturity where mediocrity finds relevance.

Since these churches are leaving the cultural past of the Church behind, they now must develop programs filled with dissertations of worldly preambles and enforcing them with entertainment styled praise and worship. Our enemy is at work using his same tactics, slowly changing the nature of churches by changing its culture but at a pace not to create any attention to the evil within it. In today's environment if anyone ask why the change, purposely deceptive narratives come from leadership saying, it is all led by the Spirit.

So, how do you change a culture? You first cease from any past mannerisms that revealed any truths or actions within its history and then deceptively tell lies carefully narrated to establish new manner of thinking not only ignorant of the past but hateful towards it.

A deception enforced by spiritual forces of darkness that brings about exactly what we now see taking place in society and churches is all a result of spiritual deception. Truths that used to be mainstay in this nation and its churched foundation have been replaced with secular humanistic teachings purposed to raise a creation above its creator. The culture of this nation and largely its churches are rooted in the fact liberty and justice for all is laid out as an integral part of its Judeo-Christian foundation.

And clearly reveals there is a covert operation taking place seen in its ability to bring change to a society and the word of God that is so deceptively like truth many follow the workers of it.

2 Peter 2:1-3 ¹ *But there were false prophets also among the people, even as there shall be false teachers among you, who privily shall bring in damnable heresies, even denying the Lord that bought them, and bring upon themselves swift destruction.* ² *And <u>many shall follow their pernicious ways</u>; by reason of whom <u>the way of truth shall be evil spoken of</u>.* ³ *And through covetousness shall they with feigned words make merchandise of you: whose judgment now of a long time lingereth not, and their damnation slumbereth not.*

Notice in verse 2 where he says the way of truth shall be evil spoken of, he is not referring to a manner of speech that slanders the word, but speaking in covert ways to make the word continue to appear true, only to cover up a deceptively evil purpose. The effects of this type of covert manner are seen in the political arenas where politicians speak exactly what the constitution says to get elected and yet once they are in, they are without any intention of upholding it.

Also look at verse 3 he says by using feigned words, this is talking about artificial substitutes, words that appear truthful but are fictitious and without power, evident by the fact they are without any ability to fulfill them. This is all part of the new "Worldly Preambles." Now being used by many churches today to bring new coverts into the congregations.

2 Tim 3:13-17 ¹³ *But <u>evil men and seducers shall wax worse and worse, deceiving</u>, and <u>being deceived</u>.* ¹⁴ *But continue thou in the things which thou hast learned and hast been assured of, knowing of whom thou hast learned them;* ¹⁵ *And that from a child thou hast known the holy scriptures, which are able to make thee wise unto salvation through faith which is in Christ Jesus.*

Paul emphasizes the importance of believers staying true to what they have learned from the scriptures as it brings about wisdom of salvation through faith. Any believer unlearned in the truths of what is revealed pertaining to works of evil taking place in the earth and the churches today will not be able to discern the perversity in it. As all scripture is given by inspiration of God.

[16] All scripture is given by inspiration of God, and is profitable for doctrine, for reproof, for correction, for instruction in righteousness: [17] That the man of God may be perfect, thoroughly furnished unto all good works.

The root word in the Greek for the word perfect in this verse is (***arti***) meaning suspended state or manner 'without change', a place where every believer should be regarding all things present in their life. Living in a time of turmoil as the end of the Church age gets closer reveals God's offspring must by revelation of truths in the word learn to discern the evil from the good, or I say Godly.

During the time of the end of the Church age it is not going to be warfare solely in the spirit realm with the devil, but with people brought to do evil through ignorance and stupidity making the battle ground much broader.

The faults that lie within churches will cause many to be void of life as God has purposed, all accomplished by pulpits turning away from spiritual truths, leaving hearts and minds deceived to do contrary to the word. As pulpits make the past traditions of ministry the mediocrity of today, they leave out spiritual issues they see no longer needed.

Thus, in an age where trends and vile emotional idealisms have more premise than truth it was also in the early Church where faults of religious piety based on platonic ideals deceived people for two millennia. And there are forms of spiritual deception yet to be seen in the order of things to come riding on an order for our extinction.

An End will Come!

I know all of this seems disheartening and hard to swallow but hold on to your faith, God is true to His word. Though our enemy has his bastions of ignorance and deceits among the Church an end to his evil shenanigans is coming with outpourings of the Spirit of God never seen before, nor ever will be again on planet earth.

Joel 2:1-11 [1] *Blow ye the trumpet in Zion, and sound an alarm in my holy mountain: let all the inhabitants of the land tremble: for <u>the day of the LORD cometh</u>, for it is nigh at hand;*

Anyone who ministers narratives fashioned for a purpose of ill truths regarding the status of the Church and God's judgments in the days before Jesus removes it from the earth is of a deceiving spirit. I say deceiving because scripture is not only aligned to the glory of His works it is also aligned to revealing the evil works that plague us. And as apparent in the fact He states a blasting alert is coming from **Zion** the spiritual pillar of truth, an alarm sounded in the high places of holiness, will be the Church.

[2] *A day of darkness and of gloominess, a day of clouds and of thick darkness, as the morning spread upon the mountains: a great people and a strong; there hath not been ever the like, neither shall be any more after it, even to the years of many generations.*

The time when the Church takes a stance on truths He revealed for its work in the days before the end, is a time when the Spirit of God goes before it leaving behind a trail of people astonished by His witness and either changed to do God's will or removed for resisting the Spirit of God.

[3] *A fire devoureth before them; and behind them a flame burneth: the land is as the garden of Eden before them, and behind them a desolate wilderness; yea, and nothing shall escape them.*

The sound of it will be greater than what was heard on the day of Pentecost, it will not be as a wind but as a force much more solid in its presence and efforts. Those who are part of it will be seen and heard as they speak with a sounding voice of truth manifesting the power of God having immediate supernatural results.

⁴ The appearance of them is as the appearance of horses; and as horsemen, so shall they run. ⁵ Like the noise of chariots on the tops of mountains shall they leap, like the noise of a flame of fire that devoureth the stubble, as a strong people set in battle array.

In amazement of what is seen fear will appear in the faces of those who have stood against God's truth, as a glorious valor among these ministers causes unity without judgment and error of the word. Mediocrity is nowhere to be found and all who fall upon a weapon of evil (words aligned to destroy them) will not be harmed or injured in a spiritual sense.

⁶ Before their face the people shall be much pained: all faces shall gather blackness. ⁷ They shall run like mighty men; they shall climb the wall like men of war; and they shall march everyone on his ways, and they shall not break their ranks: ⁸ Neither shall one thrust another; they shall walk everyone in his path: and when they fall upon the sword, they shall not be wounded.

Nothing can stand in the path of such a supernatural force that is so great the heavens are affected by what they do. Every possible path for a righteous work to be done by an offspring of God for a witness and testimony of truths from the word will be set before them. And nothing or no one will escape the effects of it as the power contained within immediately does the will of God.

⁹ They shall run to and fro in the city; they shall run upon the wall, they shall climb up upon the houses; they shall enter in at the windows like a thief. ¹⁰ The earth shall quake before them; the heavens shall tremble: the sun and the moon shall be dark, and the stars shall withdraw their shining:

It is the word and the Spirit bringing deliverance, repentance, and salvation to the creation all presented through the Church, Christ body of believers aligned to the will of the Father in heaven. This is all spelled out in scriptures written into the New Testament by Paul and prophetically legitimized in the Old Testament.

[11] And the LORD shall utter his voice before his army: for his camp is very great: for he is strong that executeth his word: for the day of the LORD is great and very terrible; and who can abide it?

Throughout the later years of the Church there has been words spoken concerning a moving of the Spirit of God through the Church to bring into alignment those who minister at the pulpits. It will be a time of cleansing unlike any other to occur that is already working in areas of the world and beginning to be seen in this nation.

Eph 5:25-27 *[25] Husbands, love your wives, even as Christ also loved the church, and gave himself for it; [26] That he might sanctify and cleanse it with the washing of water by the word, [27] That he might present it to himself a glorious church, not having spot, or wrinkle, or any such thing; but that it should be holy and without blemish.*

In the aftermath of its work will be a glorious Church without the iniquities of its past in unity of Spirit to complete what has been prophesied over all its occupants. Those unwilling to repent of their errors and miss leadings of God's children will find their ordnance removed and office revoked, others willing to defy God's will may find themselves in a much worse position.

Psalm 96:13 *[13] Before the LORD: for he cometh, for he cometh to judge the earth: he shall judge the world with righteousness, and the people with his truth.*

Believers must know the Lord will not defy His Father's will and accept this new era of blending worldly ideals with the truth of the word. Thus, judgment occurs to remove all evils and wickedness from the pulpits so that His siblings are free to receive all truths He has determined they should know, and not what man has determined for centuries.

1 Cor 6:9 ⁹ Know ye not that the unrighteous shall not inherit the kingdom of God? Be not deceived: neither fornicators, nor idolaters, nor adulterers, nor effeminate, nor abusers of themselves with mankind

The greatest deception upon creation is any work to prevent you from knowing truth about God and what He has done and the work of the Lord Jesus Christ to remove any sin that keeps you from being a child of God.

Your enemy the devil is the true deceiver, and he knows well how to do it, but the word and the Spirit reveal his evil tactics and devises, so believers in Christ must not be found trusting in his words. Nothing is being withheld from those who trust in the Lord, and every aspect of why deception must be avoided is made known and the way of righteousness revealed.

1 Cor 15:32-34 (GW) ³² If I have fought with wild animals in Ephesus, what have I gained according to the way people look at things? If the dead are not raised, "Let's eat and drink because tomorrow we're going to die!" ³³ Don't let anyone deceive you. Associating with bad people will ruin decent people. ³⁴ Come back to the right point of view, and stop sinning. Some people don't know anything about God. You should be ashamed of yourselves.

Even those you fellowship with could be of a deceitful manner, which is revealed in whether they believe that it is only by the word and the Spirit are the way to truths from God, or not.

Gal 6:2-8 [2] *Bear ye one another's burdens, and so fulfil the law of Christ.* [3] *For if a man think himself to be something, when he is nothing, <u>he deceiveth himself</u>.* [4] *But let every man prove his own work, and then shall he have rejoicing in himself alone, and not in another.* [5] *For every man shall bear his own burden.* [6] *<u>Let him that is taught in the word communicate unto him that teacheth in all good things</u>.*

The revealed truth here is that anyone who is taught in the word should be of a right manner of communication with those who are teaching without any deceit in their intentions.

[7] *<u>Be not deceived</u>; God is not mocked: for whatsoever a man soweth, that shall he also reap.* [8] *For he that soweth to his flesh shall of the flesh reap corruption; but he that soweth to the Spirit shall of the Spirit reap life everlasting.*

This is all very important for the believer to know as everything that comes from those in leadership may not always be of the truth or without deceit. Since the enemy is capable of deceiving anyone including those who fill positions of reverence in the local church.

It does not mean everyone in leadership is deceitful but tells us we must be of a mind to take what they speak and funnel it through the scriptures by the help of the Holy Spirit.

2 Tim 3:13-15 [13] *But <u>evil men and seducers shall wax worse and worse</u>, <u>deceiving</u>, <u>and being deceived</u>.* [14] *But continue thou in the things which thou hast learned and hast been assured of, knowing of whom thou hast learned them;* [15] *And that from a child thou hast <u>known the holy scriptures</u>, which are <u>able to make thee wise unto salvation through faith which is in Christ Jesus</u>.*

The day of truth is upon us as right now the world has gone into an ideological stupor where everywhere there are people saying the things wholly contrary to the truth for a purpose of deception.

This is a time when only those who know what God's word says about it will find peace and comfort amid the tribulations caused by all these evil deceptions. Even the final events revealed in scripture show us deception is the way of evil and those who use it to either control or destroy are headed for an event that will determine their fate forever.

Rev 19:20 *²⁰ And the beast was taken, and with him the false prophet that wrought miracles before him, with which <u>he deceived them that had received the mark of the beast</u>, and <u>them that worshipped his image</u>. These both were cast alive into a lake of fire burning with brimstone.*

CHAPTER TWO
Religious Prospering

As the early Church moved away from its Jewish foundations it found control in the platonic of allegories and paganisms rooted in plagiarized philosophies. Which as I said, became the roots for many religious contents, though they were not founded upon a literal biblical sense. Those leaders found a nuance within this foundation that brought with it a sense of control and as divisions and sects of various testaments popped up all over the place each stated they believe to be better.

However, along with this an ignorance appeared to a liability of faith God meant to be developed within them. What was formally discerned by Israel in the early days as from an all-powerful God is now discerned by leadership as whether relevant to any religious and or denominational statutes sustaining this newfound control. And as leadership sought to prosper, they invoked doctrinal ideals while opting out of truth about diversity of spiritual activity.

Mediocrity brought about by this philosophical era is still here today strewn among all the varied doctrinal elements of the churches of the body of Christ seen in the fact each has drawn out tenants of faith for protecting beliefs inherent to its own defined doctrine.

Such articles reveal there is witness of a spirit of division that often presents a misrepresented Christ sacrifice for creation. These agencies promote ordinances that often create one of the greatest works of deception, concerning God's plan for His spiritual lineage living by dominion on this earth.

I am sure you have heard about Adam's treasonous act that had relinquished a sovereignty of power endowed to him by God, and rendered humanity's spiritual dominion to our enemy via a curse. This spiritual dominion is to be A *dominance of power,* that is active on the earth over all that God declared to be under it, and still present and purposed to do according to His will today.

Gen 1:28 *(ASV) And God blessed them: and God said unto them, Be fruitful, and multiply, and replenish the earth, and subdue it; and* ***have dominion*** *<u>over the fish of the sea</u>, and <u>over the birds of the heavens</u>, and <u>over every living thing that moveth upon the earth</u>.*

The sovereignty of God presents a supernatural force revealing an authority and power to enact upon whatever He chooses. Adams actions transferred this power to the curse which rendered humanity under an influence of an evil natured enemy, Satan.

Therefore, this spiritual dominion is to be exerted here by His subordinate offspring and to have a measure of sovereignty passed upon all who participate for a continual operation of blessings upon His creation. But there is one exclusion to the power to be exercised in this dominance it is humanity itself, as no one has rights to exert any authority over another person's will.

The Battle for Control

Beyond humanity's purpose of procreation lies an eternal one God perceived to be at work in this earth that requires one to be fully perceptive of since there is this manner of spirit those He proclaims as His lineage are to characterize on earth.

The fact it is to be aligned with the Spirit of God as revealed by truths all believers must know, is what is written as paramount to a heaven occupation. The various denominational and religious sects have prospered by maintaining control of dogmas founded upon platonic doctrines born out of egos and desire to control occupants.

Many religious transcripts of the Catholic Church are for the most part aligned to the compassion and caring of Christ for His creation, but within are tenants of faith in conflict with spiritual senses. Any doctrinal precept to bind human nature and then promote an ill-mannered sexual characteristic to hide it, is evil by all perverse pretenses.

This issue of leadership demanding church clergy self-impose celibacy to delusional ideas of spirituality is nowhere in the confines of scripture and had to be written into their version of a doctrinal contrast so the context for a forced celibacy would be accepted. This one idealistic doctrine has helped to create in our society today a whole sect of pedophiles who now by activist means want to make it an acceptable sexual plight of our children.

The Catholic Church still exhorts this perversity that at its core defies the creative purpose of humanity. This kind of ideological control has gone on for centuries, so are churches ever going to do something to bring a stop to this evil done by their own leadership?

I know scriptures reveal celibates were among the early church and regarded marriage as not relevant in contrast to spiritual intent. But many were either forced as in early days or chose to be as such in fulfilling a ministry calling.

However, Jesus himself was the one who emphasized marriage as the preferred accommodation for any sexual interactions of males and females complimenting each by a life God deemed from such covenant unions.

Today we have organizations aligning control through enforced doctrines that develop a disdain of truths as the pulpits spend time lamenting over influences of scriptural doxology.

A discuss of the history of the Church is difficult to express since far reaching tentacles of this controlling spirit travail in much of the Church's denominational hierarchy today. Even the plight of the Jews from the church as the end of the second century closed was itself an orchestrated event by leadership desiring to do what was needed to gain control over its occupants.

Today this is aspect of control is not hidden but in plain view and clearly seen by looking at the lack of freedom the Spirit of God has in this day of ministry, as He is no longer at the spiritual head of pulpit activity in many churches.

Even an issue as clear in scripture as the trinity or what some call the triune Godhead is controversy among these various sects. Though the word clearly reveals it is comprised of three separate personalities in a spiritual unity that reveals God the Father, Jesus the Son, and the Holy Spirit, it has been made to be confounding.

As churches quibble over scriptural issues, the ignorance for the common congregant continues to prevail concerning truth. But in the annals of knowledge and understanding from scripture we find it is all held together by the Spirit of God, and no denomination or body of elite spiritual doters can convey their own doctrinal ideals. Simply put if what was sanctioned by God is for His creation and none other, it makes our existence not related to a spirit of control but to a God who created us.

Thus, it is important for believers to remember, it is the *spirit* of a person that is born again or made alive again when they accept the Lord Jesus as savior. And that it is something no denomination or any leadership has control over since it supernaturally occurs by the Holy Spirit and the word of God.

John 1:12-13 But as many as received him, to <u>them gave He power to become the sons of God</u>, even to them that believe on his name: [13] *<u>Which were born</u>, not of blood, nor of the will of the flesh, nor of the will of man, but <u>of God</u>.*

No one is saved by any orchestrated work of ministry but only by faith in the word. God, is going to remain who He is and is not in any way subject to anyone else's manner of spiritual law nor any ruling authorities of darkness, and neither are those who are His offspring under such forces of control.

This means accountability for a child of God, is to discern if leadership is by the Spirit of God lending to the truth of scripture as revealed for ones right of maturity. Especially since a certain issue has risen in the church today where we have a deluge of ministers vainly intrigued by things like climatic exposure. And are aspiring to reach others by using techniques to appeal to *souls* focused upon the global climate trend of the day.

Is this an error? I say it is an excuse to not do as the Spirit of God historically has done in the churches of the past. Since true spiritual sense about the earth and how it is made starts and ends with the word as revealed by the Holy Spirit and nothing humanity does can ever render the same affects.

Isa 45:18 (MSG) GOD, Creator of the heavens— he is, remember, God. Maker of earth— he put it on its foundations, built it from scratch. He didn't go to all that trouble to just leave it empty, nothing in it. He made it to be lived in. This GOD says: "I am GOD, the one and only.

Today's globalist, think the earth is under humanity's control and through activist activity imply they are the only ones who have a right to impose upon individual lives evil ideals such as our own self-extinction.

Churches who promote this volatility of thinking are under an influence by spiritual forces of darkness that reveals an evil intent is being held in the heart.

Along with this are pulpits who see praise and worship as an inciteful rise for emotional tenures as they teeter on ignorance of true praise and worship by the Spirit. Because God, who is blessed by the praises of His people says He will inhabit praise, so when a spiritual elevation occurs by the presence of the Holy Spirit, a true habitation appears.

Psalm 22:3 But thou art holy, O thou that inhabitest the praises of Israel.

The ministry of praise and worship is a strong instrument when promoting emotional via's, but it must be done under auspice of not appearing expressionistic by those involved. However, in today's characterization of praise and worship I see an ignorance flowing in many churches where they now use dark arenas, hard lighting, and worldly edification as the way to appeal to the human soul. And by adding backlit stages and large LED screens they can present an exonerated outer limit of worship.

John 4:24 *(AMP)* *God is a Spirit (a spiritual Being) and those who worship Him must worship Him in spirit and in truth (reality).*

If humanity is the only part of creation mentioned in scripture capable of revealing His image, an understanding of why we are made in such a way must be perceived. The purpose of praise and worship is for us to better intercourse with Him regarding us as His offspring.

The fact an exodus is occurring simply reveals life in Christ today is to accommodate much of the world's ways. So, it does not take a ministerial genius to see what is happening because of a lack of truth and Spirit.

The fact God said those who are His spiritual offspring are in His words as gods, does not refer to believers as gods as He is, but gods in the fact He created them to express His authority by a place within His eternal hierarchy.

*Ps 8:4-9 What is man that You are mindful of him, and the son of [earthborn] man that You care for him? ⁵ Yet <u>You have made him but a little lower than God</u> [or heavenly beings], and You have crowned him with glory and honor. ⁶ You **made him to have dominion over the works of Your hands**; You have put all things under his feet: ⁷ All sheep and oxen, yes, and the beasts of the field, ⁸ The birds of the air, and the fish of the sea, and whatever passes along the paths of the seas. ⁹ O Lord, our Lord, how excellent (majestic and glorious) is Your name in all the earth!*

A spiritual dominion from a sovereign position that oversees blessings He decreed for the poor, the fatherless, the afflicted, and the destitute is only going to occur by believers who are as He is in *spirit* and *soul*. Making it clear He created them to be His spiritual representatives placed in a hierarchy that operates by His authority. So, believers are *Spiritually Subordinate Offspring" who exercise His authority so that all blessings He purposes will appear on earth.*

Now, when was the last time you as a believer heard a message about your sovereign rights as a child of an Almighty God holding position within His spiritual hierarchy? Though there are continuing spiritual battles against evils at work in both the earth and in the atmosphere above it. He has handed much of it over to His offspring to do judgment upon by the Holy Spirit.

God who is a spirit unseen in natural form chooses to appear in some celestial manner, and His nature is perfect in every aspect of knowledge and understanding, and His wisdom is inherently seen in principles He governs himself by.

He reveals attributes of Agape love, as it makes relevant what believers need to know as to why they love and desire to be His spiritual offspring. Thus, exalting God by emotional experiences not by a spiritual relationship makes Him appear just as the world, dramatic and often vile in His intent towards humanity.

The reason many cultivated evils have entered the church today is truth is easily removed by societal and cultural dramas. It is only His true offspring who will declare and reveal the glory of God in this earth through ministry of Jesus Christ, as His Son.

John 8:44-45 *[44] Ye are of your father the devil, and the lusts of your father ye will do. He was a murderer from the beginning, and abode not in the truth, because there is no truth in him. When he speaketh a lie, he speaketh of his own: for he is a liar, and the father of it. [45] And because I tell you the truth, ye believe me not.*

Like it or not it is the devil who is the father of lies capable of deceptions of truths, who also appeals to one's soul, using words he has carefully chosen filled with evil intentions.

Rom 10:9-10 (AMP) *Because if you acknowledge and confess with your lips that Jesus is Lord and in your heart believe (adhere to, trust in, and rely on the truth) that God raised Him from the dead, you will be saved. [10] For with the heart a person believes (adheres to, trusts in, and relies on Christ) and so is justified (declared righteous, acceptable to God), and with the mouth he confesses (declares openly and speaks out freely his faith) and confirms [his] salvation.*

The devil by deception manages to be the one in authority over many a believer no longer under the nurturing of the Spirit of God by pulpits they aspire to. Every believer's confession of faith in Christ, is being challenged by cultural meandering and an inclusive passivism purposely meant to leave out every important fact of life.

Scripture says we are made new creations in Christ and old things have died, and all things new are of God, having received a new life, a living *spirit*. Jesus, came as the Son of Man and was crucified for your sins, but <u>He is the Son of God</u> in all terms of righteousness, therefore no blended homiletics of world and word should affect the salvation of your *soul* accounted in Him.

2 Cor 5:17-19 (NKJV) Therefore, if anyone is in Christ, <u>he is a new creation</u>; old things have passed away; behold, all things have become new. [18] *Now all things are of God, who has reconciled us to Himself through Jesus Christ, and has given us the ministry of reconciliation,* [19] *that is, that God was in Christ reconciling the world to Himself, not imputing their trespasses to them, and has committed to us the word of reconciliation.*

Any believer who presents a true witness by testimony of a now reconciled life through Jesus Christ reveals it did not occur by any denomination or religious organization, but only by the word and Spirit. Since believers are redeemed, spiritual offspring positioned in the family of God, they hold a hierarchical spot in the realm of the spirit, not in a physical term. And since *spirit* and *soul* are parts of us as created by God, they are to be conscious of all truths He reveals.

Rom 5:5 [5] *And hope maketh not ashamed; because <u>the love of God is shed abroad in our hearts by the Holy Ghost which is given unto us</u>.*

All knowledge of things the Spirit of God is at work in is, so we have perception of them. Take the Agape love of God that now abides within believers it cannot mature unless they know who they are in Christ void of any effects of past sins. Most of the tenants of faith formed by religious organizations are for the most part a continuum of truth regarding Christ and Him crucified.

But an ordinance of control is laced within creating a pathway for evils to have influence on those born again as part of God's spiritual *heritage* and *lineage.* No one can ever be made an offspring of God, by any manmade servanthood, but by the Spirit they are born again to grow and know all things pertaining to them as they are now a part of the family of God. Thus, fulfilling a representative purpose He has ordained.

1 Cor 2:12-16 *(NKJV)* *Now we have received, not the spirit of the world, but the Spirit who is from God, that we might know the things that have been freely given to us by God.* *13* *These things we also speak, not in words which man's wisdom teaches but which the Holy Spirit teaches, comparing spiritual things with spiritual.*

The more the world's ways get mixed with kingdom principles the more unnatural the spiritual precepts of truth become causing voids in actual discernment. All things that arrive from the *spirit* realm are not revealed by natural sight, but revealed by revelation that comes by the Spirit and the word.

14 *But the natural man does not receive the things of the Spirit of God, for they are foolishness to him; nor can he know them, because they are spiritually discerned.*

The natural man is an unbeliever but those who receive such spiritually discerned revelation are those born again by the Spirit of God. But leadership by someone having strong influence on you might not have the same intent and concern as God for you, thus they might control or influence you working out your salvation.

It is important believers have knowledge of this fact as it reveals any possible control or influence over their path of faith has a ramification regarding an eternal destiny. But herein lies a key to knowing whether those in their aspired leadership are of a right spirit or not.

It is to be discerned by how leadership exercises control either by use of worldly ideals and trends, or by scripturally based truths that give freedom to the Spirit of God. It is a believer's responsibility to judge themselves so that their salvation, remains their right as a part of their inheritance, and is not in jeopardy by ignorance of such truths.

Since many denominations are held together by control over the tenants they oversee, they hide certain truths while proselytizing a form of salvation they deem is relevant. Not every believer has a liberty in Christ to embrace and accept the Spirit of God who personally sees to their wellbeing of spirit and soul by the word.

Therefore, believers are to be of the mind of Christ free of any bondage to religious or denominational control affecting a righteous standing with God.

15 But he who is spiritual judges all things, yet he himself is rightly judged by no one. 16 For "who has known the mind of the LORD that he may instruct Him?" But we have the mind of Christ.

Why do Evil Spirits Prevail in the Church?

There are many areas where evil tendencies appear present, but one is front and center in today's work of ministry. In a recent article there was an announcement of the split up of the Methodist church. The article rendered it occurred because of an ongoing internal battle amongst leadership over allowing LGBTQ modernist to fulfill roles of leadership within the Methodist organization.

This is all centered around various statements by those who see the love of God as triumph over His word, meaning to them it does not matter if what one is doing is sin in His sight, He loves you and that is all there is to it you can do what you want. The simplicity in this is not as stated, God does love the person, but not the person's sin and He never will.

But such truth does not detour the aspirations of those who see sexually biased lifestyles as higher forms of social unity. Because there is always a sexual dark side associated to evil spirits and idols of false gods brought on by ignorance. And has been around since humanity's early days promoted by the devil. As idols like Molech required sacrifices mainly consisting of first-born children which at times was merely ceremonial but often a living sacrifice of a child was thrown into a fire pit.

Lev 20:3 [3] *And I will set my face against that man, and will cut him off from among his people; because he hath <u>given of his seed unto Molech</u>, to defile my sanctuary, and to profane my holy name.*

There were two false deities worshipped in the Old Testament period who were principal figures in promoting sexual heresies by Israel and Judah. Molech represented the male perspective of this, and Ashtoreth represented the female perspective, together beliefs in them were instrumental in promoting spiritual atrocities.

A believer must have knowledge and understanding of where the origin of any evil lies and how it can enter churches, which is often through leadership's disdaining of truths.

2 Peter 2:1-9 [(MSG)] [1] *But there were also <u>lying prophets</u> among the people then, just as there will be <u>lying religious teachers</u> among you. They'll smuggle in destructive divisions, pitting you against each other—biting the hand of the One who gave them a chance to have their lives back! They've put themselves on a fast downhill slide to destruction,*

Sexual perversity appearing in churches is a designed plan of the enemy, but there is likelihood of it not being there if leadership was attuned to the working of the Spirit of God. Sin has no authority over truth contained within scripture, however, take away truth, and any lie you want can be dribbled out and promoted as the truth.

² but not before they recruit a crowd of <u>mixed-up followers who can't tell right from wrong</u>. They give the way of truth a bad name.

Pay careful attention this is applied to you as a child of God. If we add to this the fact for centuries leadership has been placated around a sense of control that prospers by religious ideals, designed to keep congregants in a confounded state of maturity. Then a path for gullible acceptance is already set. You can see this in the way many have become emotionally fixated upon leadership promoting love as sole authority.

³ They're only out for themselves. <u>They'll say anything</u>, anything, that sounds good to exploit you. They won't, of course, get by with it. They'll come to a bad end, for God has never just stood by and let that kind of thing go on.

Though God's love for you is vital to your life He will not love your sins. Look at the below scripture every godless thing will come to an end as God will not change His position on sins.

⁴ <u>God didn't let the rebel angels off the hook</u>, but jailed them in hell till Judgment Day. ⁵ <u>Neither did he let the ancient ungodly world off</u>. He wiped it out with a flood, rescuing only eight people— Noah, the sole voice of righteousness, was one of them.

God is not as merciless by nature as some would have us think but He does judge sin and only remission of it and repentance from it brings a righteous position through Jesus Christ.

⁶ God decreed destruction for the cities of Sodom and Gomorrah. A mound of ashes was all that was left—<u>grim warning to anyone bent on an ungodly life</u>.

Sexual perversity is a by-product of spiritual ignorance, and it helps to hide many evil intentions. This is what is going on today in churches, who's leadership accepts abortion, homosexuality, and the ills of gender identity perversion.

⁷ But that good man Lot, <u>driven nearly out of his mind by the sexual filth and perversity, was rescued</u>. ⁸ Surrounded by moral rot day after day after day, that righteous man was in constant torment. ⁹ So God knows how to rescue the godly from evil trials. And he knows how to hold the feet of the wicked to the fire until Judgment Day.

Lot was under torment of *soul* because of the severity of sexual perversion going on around him. We have congregants today who are also under torment of *soul* because of leadership's ignorance of truth about good and evil. This is a spiritual torment because they exhort abortion, homosexuality, and gender neutrality as acceptable sins, it is as though each has no spiritual ramification.

There is nothing, and I repeat nothing, in the annals of scripture to justify taking away an individual spirit life conceived by a process no one in humanity has a right to interfere with, since God himself created and ordained this as a way of procreating life.

The real-life essence in every individual is the *spirit* which at conception begins anew and is destined to become exactly who they will grow up to be as part of humanity. Therefore, anyone supporting abortion is clearly void of such truth or they willingly deny God has created the spiritual element of all males and females He says are born in three parts clearly seen illustrated in His word.

1 Thess 5:23 *²³ And the very God of peace sanctify you wholly; and I pray God your whole <u>spirit</u> and <u>soul</u> and <u>body</u> be preserved blameless unto the coming of our Lord Jesus Christ.*

Ministries and churches who support this evil act of murder are the same as the religious leaders of Israel in ***Isaiah 28:*** all under a spiritual stupor, that in this case is one that is murderous and evil. Sustaining missed guised love while holding onto resolute ignorance based on their own liberated senselessness is not acceptable to God.

There are scriptural facts that reveal the truth, if the <u>spirit</u> of a person leaves their body it will not continue to live, as the *spirit* is the very essence of life within them. You also need to know that wherever the *spirit* goes so goes the *soul*, which is viewed as one's consciousness, intellect, emotions, and feelings, etc.

James 2:26 ²⁶ *For as the <u>body</u> without the spirit is <u>dead</u>, so faith without works is dead also.*

Your *spirit* is the real you and you have a *soul* and live in a *body* and nothing anyone does can change this. The fact that you were a spirit dead to sin before God, you were made alive again through faith in Jesus Christ.

Abortion reveals the difference between two issues, one that deals with dead spirits (those still in sin and without God) the other that deals with (spirits whose body has been destroyed) taking away a habitation of a life God planned for them to live. The first may be a prominent concerning social elite within society but the second is a paramount evil as seen in the annals of heaven.

Truths pertaining to abortion of life as He has determined it to be within scripture is far and away more relevant to God than church leaderships spiritually ignorant killing innocent fetuses. The choice of life in the hearts of those who see a fetus as just a mass of cells fails in respect to truth, and yet they see life from a similar manner of cell tissues when talking about animals and their right to live.

These people will valiantly fight to preserve the right of a dog or cat to be born, but vehemently deny a right for a human fetus to be birthed. Clearly there is a wicked and perverse thinking promoted by spirits of ancient idols who today reign in the hearts and minds of many in society and the Church. Thus, a question you should ask yourself, how does such ignorance run its course through a Church, that is supposed to be the most right-minded organization on earth?

The answer is too simple! As it has to do with this manner of control of congregants and ignorantly breeding mediocrity as stated earlier. Those early platonic allegories created voids of truth that are still present today continuing to lay foundation for an ignorance to prevail favoring those seeking power and control.

However, God does not speak for the purpose of promoting an ignorance or mediocrity among His offspring He speaks truth for the purpose of transforming them.

Prov 8:8-10 *(AMP) All the words of my mouth are righteous (upright and in right standing with God); there is nothing contrary to truth or crooked in them. ⁹They are all plain to him who understands [and opens his heart], and right to those who find knowledge [and live by it]. ¹⁰Receive my instruction in preference to [striving for] silver, and knowledge rather than choice gold,*

Humanity may be plagued by its own weaknesses of mind and heart, but God still promotes truth. Any who seek praise from others of authority and power to sustain an ego ridden with ignorance are selfishly led about by evils they deny even exists.

There is the day of reality coming that will reveal all of this and it will be by a wave of revelation having such spiritual magnitude the Church will be immediately enlighten to its evil stance against a sovereign position of hierarchy God planned to exist.

You Must Rebuke Ignorance

Though there are churches who fall into many of the categories mentioned all are not as dysfunctional in the spiritual sense, as we might think. Some churches have in the past years seen the wayward trends toward more worldly consciousness within ministry and are earnestly seeking to insure anyone attending today is clearly about doing things as when ministry was evident by the Spirit and word.

Acts 4:13-14 [13] *Now when they saw the boldness of Peter and John, and* perceived that they were unlearned and ignorant men, *they marvelled; and they took knowledge of them, that they had been with Jesus.* [14] *And beholding the man which was healed standing with them, they could say nothing against it.*

The ignorance as referenced here of Peter and John is not about scriptural understanding but about religious authority and its right to impose some manner of control or governance upon the truth. It was clear these church magistrates who saw this once crippled man now exerting an ability to do what he could not do since birth, presented a situation they were not sure how to handle.

Though the event revealed truth no one's ignorance could even overrule, they still found it to be unacceptable, because it challenged their authority and control. In them offering no sense of explanation clearly revealed they could not deny what happened but for the sake of authority had to impose a liberal senselessness of control on Peter and John regardless of the truth.

Rom 1:11-15 [11] *For I long to see you, that I may impart unto you some spiritual gift, to the end ye may be established;* [12] *That is, that I may be comforted together with you by the mutual faith both of you and me.* [13] *Now* I would not have you ignorant*, brethren, that oftentimes I purposed to come unto you, (but was let hitherto,) that I might have some fruit among you also, even as among other Gentiles.* [14] *I am debtor both to the Greeks, and to the Barbarians; both to the wise, and to the unwise.* [15] *So, as much as in me is, I am ready to preach the gospel to you that are at Rome also.*

Paul's inference of ignorance in this scripture is not in tune to any religious authority as we saw before, but God's will regarding everyone and the truth He has revealed. He makes this statement in considering an opportunity to minister the gospel to those believers who were in Rome.

Rom 10:1-9 *[1] Brethren, my heart's desire and prayer to God for Israel is, that they might be saved. [2] For I bear them record that they have a zeal of God, but not according to knowledge. [3] For <u>they being ignorant of God's righteousness</u>, and going about to establish their own righteousness, have not submitted themselves unto the righteousness of God. [4] For Christ is the end of the law for righteousness to everyone that believeth*

Paul speaking to Jews who were not ignorant of who God was but clearly ignorant of His righteousness and the impact it was to have on a whole nation He chose to save through the Messiah, Jesus Christ. As hard as Israel tried to present a righteousness before Him it was without faith in the one who will ultimately save them.

1 Cor 12:1-3 *[1] Now concerning spiritual gifts, brethren, <u>I would not have you ignorant</u>. [2] Ye know that ye were Gentiles, carried away unto these dumb idols, even as ye were led. [3] Wherefore I give you to understand, that no man speaking by the Spirit of God calleth Jesus accursed: and that no man can say that Jesus is the Lord, but by the Holy Ghost.*

There is knowledge and understanding of the purpose for these nine spiritual gifts Paul goes on to detail in verses 4 through 11 of *1 Cor 12:* it reveals the importance each of them has in every aspect of a believer's life. Since these are venues by which supernatural power will manifest by the Holy Spirit.

The fact scriptural ignorance is today among many congregants regarding intent and concern the Father has for knowing these gifts and how they still operate, is astounding when we consider His word has not changed.

2 Peter 3:3-5, 8 *[3] Knowing this first, that there shall come in the last days scoffers, walking after their own lusts, [4] And saying, Where is the promise of his coming? for since the fathers fell asleep, all things continue as they were from the beginning of the creation. [5]*

For <u>this they willingly are ignorant of</u>, that by the word of God the heavens were of old, and the earth standing out of the water and in the water/ [8] But, beloved, <u>be not ignorant of this one thing</u>, that one day is with the Lord as a thousand years, and a thousand years as one day.

Where there is evidence of ignorance there is often a denial of truth that underlies an evil intent. As Peter reveals this ignorance of the creation illustrated in the book of Genesis, he emphasizes there will be a change in the day God judges humanity's sins.

The word of God is filled with every truth believer's ever need while here on planet earth. And any ignorance standing against such knowing is a plague of injustice brought about by an enemy who is without power, and any who would prosper by a doctrinal control, means they would rather have power than knowledge of truth.

Lev 4:13-15 (MSG) [13] *"<u>If the whole congregation sins unintentionally (through ignorance) by straying from one of the commandments of GOD that must not be broken, they become guilty even though no one is aware of it</u>.*

Ignorance is never an excuse to do things scripture says you are not to do, as any quilt or judgment that results from it is still being accounted. But God who is merciful has given instruction on how to be free of such quilt and/or judgment.

Acts 17:29-31 [29] *Forasmuch then as <u>we are the offspring of God</u>, we ought not to think that the Godhead is like unto gold, or silver, or stone, graven by art and man's device. [30] And the times of this ignorance God winked at; but <u>now commandeth all men every where to repent</u>: [31] Because <u>he hath appointed a day</u>, in the which <u>he will judge the world in righteousness by that man whom he hath ordained</u>; whereof he hath given assurance unto all men, in that he hath raised him from the dead.*

41

While God did not get hysterical over the fact the ignorance of humanity at a point in time saw Him as just another idol for them to worship, He eventually settled on a day He would bring judgment upon all by the one who was raised from the dead, Jesus Christ, His Son.

Repentance is not just about saying you repent of sin or evil, it is about you living in a way that such things no longer have effect on your *spirit*, *soul*, or *body*. Another reason why righteousness is the ordained stature of every offspring of God.

Today's denominations and religious organizations continue to thrive on ignorance of the believers who attend as it presents them in a stature of power and authority not from the word but doctrines of men. This is an abuse of a believer's rights as mentioned before because every son and daughter of God are in His sight, as redeemed adopted children having the same rights as Christ, His first born.

Eph 1:3-14 *³ Blessed be the God and Father of our Lord Jesus Christ, who hath blessed us with all spiritual blessings in heavenly places in Christ: ⁴ According as he hath chosen us in him before the foundation of the world, that we should be holy and without blame before him in love:*

The fact believers are an offspring of God through faith in Jesus Christ places them in a position or stature that is holy and without blame, this stature was chosen to be theirs before the foundations of this world were ever laid down.

⁵ Having predestinated us unto the adoption of children by Jesus Christ to himself, according to the good pleasure of his will, ⁶ To the praise of the glory of his grace, wherein he hath made us accepted in the beloved. ⁷ In whom we have redemption through his blood, the forgiveness of sins, according to the riches of his grace;

A believer's status before God is not just one being counted as holy and blameless in Christ, but one that is far more relevant as they are now legally affirmed as God's son or daughter. This is not the same type of legal procedure that we have in the natural for one's adoption of a child. This adoption is spiritually foundational and is empowered by the authority of a lineage (*line of descendants of a particular ancestor*) God has deemed to be His own.

What I have seen, is it is what a believer does not know that will at times cause them to find comfort in this mediocrity as ignorance placates their status.

⁸ Wherein he hath abounded toward us in all wisdom and prudence; ⁹ Having made known unto us the mystery of his will, according to his good pleasure which he hath purposed in himself: ¹⁰ That in the dispensation of the fulness of times he might gather together in one all things in Christ, both which are in heaven, and which are on earth; even in him: ¹¹ <u>In whom also we have obtained an inheritance</u>, being predestinated according to the purpose of him who worketh all things <u>after the counsel of his own will</u>:

However, scripture clearly reveals He is not intent on keeping us ignorant of the truth He has laid down for all His children. Your inheritance (*something that comes or belongs to one by reason of birth*) is in Christ situated in the realm of His kingdom to be handed on to those He sees as rightly in a heritage He deems fulfilled.

¹² That we should be to the praise of his glory, who first trusted in Christ. ¹³ In whom ye also trusted, after that ye heard the word of truth, the gospel of your salvation: in whom also after that ye believed, ye were sealed with that holy Spirit of promise, ¹⁴ Which is <u>the earnest of our inheritance until the redemption of the purchased possession</u>, unto the praise of his glory.

If you as a believer fully understand what these scriptures tell you then you are not under the oversight of those who would desire to keep you ignorant of such truth.

So, as you rebuke ignorance and personally spend time to find out what He says by the truth you read and the work of the Holy Spirit. There will be a reality as to who you are and why you are to prosper, (spiritually), as you are one of those Jesus has made a son or daughter of His Father, siblings rightly heired to eternal promises He has made.

CHAPTER THREE

The Dark Age of Israel and the Church

There is an era of humanity's history we need to look at to help us get knowledge and understanding of how long something like this spiritual mediocrity has plagued believers. The treatment of the Jews by the Church and society during an era of great tribulation helps us to learn how a period of spiritual intolerance helped the Church to change its position on Israel and the truth. Many of the following paragraphs are taken from a book titled "Religion in A Handbasket" where I write about the atrocities that occurred during and after this dark period.

Now most people have no idea of the evils that came upon the Jews during the period of the Crusades 1096-1291 AD, a time when Jewish populations became riddled with accounts of suffering and death as the Crusades took on a holier than though appearance. We can start with the Jewish communities living in northern territories of Germany and France who suffered tragedy as nearly a third of them were murdered during the first campaigns of the Crusades. And Jews still living in or around Jerusalem during the symbolic rampages also suffered as they found themselves under ridicule and expulsion with thousands slaughtered by self-righteous deliverers.

In one event alone estimates of 900-3000 died due to the fact they were locked inside Synagogues to try and survive the suffrage, unfortunately they were set on fire killing all inside. And reports say all the while the crusaders were marching outside holding up crosses and singing Christ, we adore thee.

The crusades led the way for many Jews to be under indictment and/or extermination, by eerily harsh episodes of servitude while suffering many dehumanizing treatments often fostered by church leadership. This caused the Jews to seek refuge from those who saw their death and suffering as merely doing God's work.

Even before the Crusades began there were accusations of the Jews made by the Church. As Pope Benedict VIII 1012-1024, came up with a theory the Jews must be made *scapegoats* for any atrocities that might occur as result of the Church or God. And to prove it, in 1021 he had a lot of Jews executed because of a hurricane and an earthquake that had occurred.

Such evils did not end there, during the **Black Death** in Europe circa 1347-1350, Jews found themselves along with many others held responsible for its occurrence. As history records the Jewish communities in both Mainz and Cologne were destroyed in 1349, along with this was an earlier event in February of that same year where the citizens of Strasbourg murdered more than 2000 Jews.

The Jewish people suffered afflictions for things they never did and over the centuries have wrongly been accused of atrocities they had nothing to do with or never occurred. One accusation made about the Jews is the ill-minded act of **Deicide** or more correctly the murdering of God. Another one is the **Blood Libel** that came later, a so-called fabricated tale told all throughout Europe and other central regions circa 1880 to about 1945. In this transcript of Jews were ill-mentioned episodes of abductions and murders of little children for rituals at Passover.

In 1478 the monarchs of the Catholic Church, Ferdinand II, and Isabella I, extensively cleansed the land to maintain the orthodoxy of the Catholic regime by enforcing a declaration that all other faiths be purged from its territorial presence. This one dynastic expulsion primarily focused upon Jews and Islamist, by episodes of piously religious authority managed to last well into the nineteenth century.

However, reports show that early on it devastated the Jewish people, as they were arrested in wholesale lots with the very first of them being burned at the stake. Over time several reports appeared estimating over 30,000 souls lost their lives during this so-called monarchial purge.

Here is a report you will not like; Martin Luther 1483-1546, is credited with Reformation, or *Christianity defined by grace through faith in Christ*, but he did not accept the Jews, most especially after they refused his offer of conversion. This resulted in him purposely devising anti-Semitic teachings that were to be ministered in the churches regarding the Jews. Though Luther is seen as the father of modern-day Christianity he possibly set the stage for a period in the history of the Jewish people that turned out to be maybe the darkest yet.

He wrote many statements about how their synagogues should be burned, homes destroyed, and all Jews deprived of prayer books, Rabbis forbidden to teach, and any/all privileges of travel revoked. This later become an epitaph of the Jewish people as Adolf Hitler saw it as justifiable cause to exterminate them.

I am fully conscious of the fact churches refuse to take up a discussion of our past regarding society's ills and Israel's trials as result of secular or religious acts of those in days gone by. But the truth pertaining to all of this is out there, and history reveals such events often repeat themselves. Actions of the past whether good or bad, are recorded so we might not make the same mistakes.

I have heard pastors tell congregants do not look at the past focus only on the future.

Darkness in Today's churches

While it is true, we should not dwell on or try to live in the past, in the confines of ministry there is a new venue appearing that can be defined by social outlines as politically correct which in truth is nothing more than an excuse for hypocritical humanistic behavior. A behavior that is becoming a governing factor regarding any truth of the word, since many pulpits are now fearful of social rebuttals.

The social activists of our day seek a defamation of anything and anyone that distinguishes good, and evil, right, or wrong, light, and dark within cyclic conversation and deny any scriptures that detail such things. This kind of activity is setting voids concerning truths essential to any growth of one's maturity both spiritual and natural, revealed by a character mediocre to foundational truth in Christ.

Thus, as pulpits set aside any literal aspects of scripture, they no longer see a need to cultivate growth and end up disdaining things God has said from the beginning. This makes them appear far more fearful of a social outburst in the parking lot than a God who created it all.

So, groundwork for spiritual mediocrity is being introduced into many believers lives to defer sound scriptural advice that could be applied to having spiritual sense about life, marriage, and faith. The messages from many pulpits today are all about a pumped-up social comradery, leading believers to do whatever seems right in the latest societal trend.

Giving a Sunday morning doxology on marriage containing a paramount usage of words rendering that homosexuality is perverted fiction, is now seen as an apostasy of the worst kind.

Activities of sexual abuse, rape, and incest are all on the rise in society and in churches, and congregants are seeing leadership at odds with any scripture about spiritual revelation. If the history of the Church during the dark ages reveals their sinful deeds, then a present order of it is here again.

Many papal indigents who served during those dark years in the Church, were viewed as sexual stepping points to a promiscuity that concerns today's Priest, Bishops, Cardinals, and congregants. And any idea sexual ignorance is solely confined to outside the churches is a stupid one at best, as much of it appears within its peer structured authority, by leadership resolved to continue such an evil among its patronage.

1 Peter 1:23 *(NKJV)* *23 having been born again, not of corruptible seed but* *incorruptible, through the word of God which lives and abides forever,*

Though scripture reveals believers are from an incorruptible seed when born again in Christ, it is hard to figure out how so much of the world's order of sexual discerning is becoming present in the churches of today. You can see it when you discern what is not an active part of ministry anymore, which is clearly the Spirit and the incorruptible word. Truths that brought the new birth in the first place to transform one's life to be as God has said, is no longer seen relevant to you being holy and without blame.

Church atmospheres of today openly pander to a more worldly oriented populace who see preaching truth about God as blasphemy of a social eudicot since many are activist of a societal sect who have no or little tolerance for it. Many pulpits are made out to be socially vitriol and/or pious, and any ministers caught supporting truth are subjected to exile and ridiculed by social media's intolerant cancel culture.

Something as simple as God declaring a man who has a wife has a good thing, and favor with the Lord is by today's cultural sight sexually dishonorable and in conflict to a liberal social eudicot.

Heb 13:4 Marriage is honourable in all, and the bed undefiled: but whoremongers and adulterers God will judge.

Prov 18:22 *(NKJV) He who finds a wife finds a good thing, And obtains favor from the LORD.*

So, for pulpits to now be politically correct there must be some scriptural decree that enables by an inclusive posture there is no excluding of same sex unions or alt gender instabilities. And added to this is there are to be no traces of whiteness, as exclusions of black are deemed as supremacy in an age of so-called tolerant races.

2 Cor 5:7 *(AMP) For <u>we walk by faith</u> [we regulate our lives and conduct ourselves by our conviction or belief respecting man's relationship to God and divine things, with trust and holy fervor; thus we walk] <u>not by sight or appearance</u>.*

While scripture is there for our direction of life and faith, pulpits rendering more and more emotionally based worldly text ride along social platforms of anxiety and anxiousness designed to stimulate a non-acceptance of God or anything Divine. Because without truth it has no ability to build stable spiritual relationship with the Father and the Son.

Setting in place an emotional via that must be kept alive by hermeneutics about life as one desires, and not truth as is in Christ, is hypocrisy in the Church. And follows the same line of thought we see concerning political candidates who use it to fallow out hearts and minds forcing people to see things from a narrated lie of others.

Gen 6:5-6 And God saw that the wickedness of man was great in the earth, and that <u>every imagination and the thoughts of his heart</u>

was only evil continually. [6] *And it repented the LORD that He had made man on the earth, and it grieved him at his heart.*

No doubt humanity has and will commit evil on its own, but a person's heart is subject to change if the truth is presented, and they see value in it for life. God did not create us to be struggling through life. This is a reason Jesus came so that anyone believing in Him as the Son of God would have life abundant both now and to come.

Issues that continue to plague churches are today so engrained in religious traditions and customs removing them can only occur by a supernatural power and/or death of the ideals or testator. Along with a spiritual exchange there must be a humility that emboldens the impartation of foundational values for life, liberty, and ministry that never changes.

The darkness in many churches we call political correctness exist by confusion promoted in society, making it a defining issue in a nation's quality of life. Today a heavy divide is along the lines of conservative and liberal seen both outside and inside the Church. Along with it a spiritual hatred and emotional distention that prevails by efforts of social media oligarchs and pundits whose ill-qualified egos summon a removal of all Christian entitlements.

None of this is happening by ignorance it is by design, as truth must be cut off, so voids occur regarding not only Christ and His Church but humanity at large. Biblical context will always contrast with political correctness, but the latter is now the exergies in many pulpits of today. As this happens time and time again, congregants become less and less faithful to any truths within the word lending to ignorance and accepting worldly mannered works.

Thus, we now have a dark aged mannerism present in a day of exaltation by ministries who are part of a Church that is now some 2000 years old in Christ. As politics or the mannerism of it deforms spiritual fellowship of believers, it becomes politicized by truths.

Even to the degree we have Christian sects deep into judgment and condemnation of those they deem are cause for an end time demise. Vilification of this statement can be seen by the actions of those in leadership within certain denominations who have stated in several written articles of late, saying the Evangelical sect of today's Church is responsible for single handedly structuring the Church's overall demise.

Such ideals reveal a gross intolerance and biased judgments that are solely based on a hatred of those who voted for Trump in 2016 and in our most recent 2020 election. Those people just happened to be Evangelicals or at least a majority are as stated. However, these articles are clearly designed to promote ill-content among the sects of the body of Christ solely because of their media structured hate for Mr. Trump and the office of the Presidency.

What is important is this reveal we now have spiritual activity of God being brought under a standard of politically correct ridicule by these church leaders, and persons of influence. That say if such activity is seen as not to align to this standard, then it is not worthy of any support by the Church. This means, if a person God chose to be elected is doing exactly what He endeavors them to do, and these indigents cannot accept such a person for who or what he or she is then an outright rebuke and criticism must occur.

What we see here is a religious character assassination of God, a trait straight out of the dark ages where papal powers and affiliates used religious and political authority to summon ridicule, judgment, and condemnation of anyone or anything not meeting standards they decreed. Could you ever imagine the Church would be in a time of apostasy where leadership believes they determine whether God is right or not in what He does? The dark ages are clearly here today.

John 6:70 *[70] Jesus answered them, Have not I chosen you twelve, and one of you is a devil?*

Jesus chose twelve who were sinners in His day and one of them acted out evil against Him, but His Father's plans were already set-in place requiring His fulfillment by faith. Therefore, the presence of evil did not change the course of things that pertained to life, death, and resurrection of His Son Jesus Christ. But a judgment fell on Judas based upon his acceptance of worldly evils by leadership.

Believers have account after account, in both the Old and New Testaments scriptures telling of those called out and or used by God to accomplish His will. And it is not surprising that not a one of them would be acceptable based on politically correct standards today's religious political doles have deemed themselves to be overseers of.

Rom 13:1-2 *(GW) 1 Every person should obey the government in power. <u>No government would exist if it hadn't been established by God</u>. <u>The governments which exist have been put in place by God</u>. 2 Therefore, <u>whoever resists the government opposes what God has established</u>. Those who resist will bring punishment on themselves.*

It is God who places leaders within certain governments and in worldly orders of power, not an overt order or oversight of man. He alone is in control of all powers and authorities that prevail on earth making our part in this an obedience and exaltation of what He does through them. Even if the one chosen is not of a manner of character seen worthy of such a position.

This present exposition by judgment of others in Christ is an A-typical choice of those who elect themselves to be worthy of such prowess by a false sense of authority. They are by a self-imposed ignorance existing in the confines of evil, and no longer under guide of the Spirit of God.

Now I am really going to talk about something some of you will not like and it is about how churches send forth sons and daughters of God into ministry that requires certain level of spiritual fortitude be present, but is never taught by that same leadership.

Rules of Darkness

Over the years I have seen many a believer sent forth to minister for no other reason than embolden the role of leadership within a denomination or ministry. And by an exergy of commandments and rules they have learned, quickly find out they are insufficient. Thus, end up ravaged by an evil enemy causing a spiritual vibrancy to be suppressed or worse removed, many winds up being no more than a pew occupier willing to offer money and fill a church roster count.

We have a large portion of the Church that has purposely been neutered in a spiritual sense, seen in the fact there no longer is a zeal to witness by the Holy Spirit. Some are so spiritually scared they have lost the will to have any witness at all of who they truly are. This is exactly what occurs when someone's life in Christ has been sacrificed for leadership's so called spiritual authority and then left for dead (in a spiritual sense) by these same encouragers.

Look I know such statements invoke ill among us, but I by my own personal experience over the last 40 years have been in both positions. And know others that started with a zeal of faith to fulfill every possible way to live for the Lord, but found themselves too overwhelmed by conflicts they were never trained to deal with. I know we always say if God calls, He equips, and this is true but equipping comes through those who are seasoned by the trials they have gone through before them.

Those who put believers in these positions of ministry and/or servitude and have done nothing to nurture their spiritual maturity in preparation for conflicts that will occur do so for peer exhortation. Not unlike the manner of rulership vibrant in the Church during the dark ages where papal holiness and bishopric alike ruled over the congregants demanding obedience to support a role of authority not of God. Most believers in that era lacked in the maturity necessary to deal with the everyday lives of those they were affecting.

While leadership conflicted over truths of scriptures about any aspects of so-called ministerial rights the then Church not only ruled over its congregants and much of the land, but hierarchy within the government gave it an imparting authority over even international influences.

The Church treated wealthy and affluent people as royalty, that is until rulership had no use for them anymore, then they were either beheaded or exiled, and no longer seen as valuable to a political or financial support. Leadership then lacked in a valued life expressed by ruling powers over all commoners due to an economical failure, that was a direct result of the Church's taxation policies.

While the past is viewed as an unfortunate time for the body of Christ it reflects on immaturity among congregations as well as its leadership, by those who purposely subjugate believers to the evil nature and/or character of an arch enemy. This is an apostacy before Christ, and as I said, one I have been on both sides of.

While in a position of leadership, I cared little for those who failed and made excuses for having no compassion toward them, telling myself they must learn how to do it by faith. I like others left them up to the devil's devices waiting for them to get it together, not caring when they went away and no longer in fellowship with me. Obviously, I saw this as no fault of my own as I was trained to view spiritual maturity as a process developed by adversity not by the word and Spirit of God.

However, I thank the Lord for forgiving me for such ignorance and immaturity while helping me to see a way to repent of it all. Today one of my responsibilities as part of the Church is spiritual nurturing and unity of others who are in Christ. Teaching them how to live as part of a family where one's failures or shortcomings are irrelevant to a growth in spiritual union God calls us to.

Since everyone in Christ is on their way to receiving promise of the Father, an eternal life and eventual occupation of a new earth is before us all. And no one has relevance above another as all are now sanctioned in Christ.

2 Cor 5:17-21 ^(GW) *Whoever is a believer in Christ is a new creation. The old way of living has disappeared. <u>A new way of living has come into existence</u>. ¹⁸ God has done all this. <u>He has restored our relationship with him through Christ</u>, and <u>has given us this ministry of restoring relationships</u>.*

The Holy Spirit's presence here reveals we are created to grow and mature into a life led by Him having faith that only comes by truth of the word. No one is respected more than another and each is held accountable for a building up of the whole body. What is important is that He holds no one's faults against them, as everyone in Christ are restored in relationship to an All-Mighty God.

¹⁹ *In other words, <u>God was using Christ to restore his relationship with humanity</u>. He didn't hold people's faults against them, and he has given us this message of restored relationships to tell others. ²⁰ Therefore, we are Christ's representatives, and through us God is calling you. We beg you on behalf of Christ to become reunited with God.*

So, can you see how spiritual mediocrity gets a foothold when leadership is not in tune to the Spirit of God? Much of it occurs when power and authority are paramount to a position of self-exaltation where they force anyone of lesser rule to be part of the order and any who refuse removed whether brother or sister or even their own parents.

There is very little clarity on this issue, but historically stated facts do reveal we are in a time where Christ's representatives are once again under an order of rulership and not relationship.

²¹ God had Christ, who was sinless, take our sin so that we might receive God's approval through him.

No one is excluded from God's family He sent His only Son Jesus to remove all fault in His creation so that anyone could be reunited into their true family heritage. But since the time of the early Church focus has been on ministry of dark age doctrines to support egos establishing scriptural correctness in a time when the Church should be at its most epic moment, spiritually.

Therefore, I believe the Lord is going to deal with this in this final hour of the Church to bring unity and spiritual harmony that surpasses even the outpouring of the Holy Spirit on the day of Pentecost. The Church's final works will bring into the kingdom a great harvest of souls by faithfulness to fulfill what Jesus declared would be in the day of His return.

Spiritual Offspring not Ministerial Offspring

Almost all believers are trained to look at Christianity through a ministerial prism regarding relationship in Christ. I know this is not a subject homiletically prepared by pulpits, but I want to make known there is a <u>religious spirit</u> putting blinders on God's children. Done to prevent real truths from being known that reveal they are of a heritage founded upon an eternal promise from God.

This is being carefully presented as spiritual activity in Christ which in the confines of its guidelines must always be anchored to some sort of ministerial event. I know this may look like I am playing down or criticizing ministry, but I assure you I am not, it is very important for you and me as parts of the family of God to fulfill all works of spiritual servitude as the body of Christ. Since no one else is going to reveal the Father and lift Jesus Christ as Lord in this world, it is a heritage and destiny as His responsible offspring who by the Holy Spirit do what He wants us to do.

However, today's believers are struggling to get their spiritual senses aware of the fact that first and foremost they are sons and daughters of God.

Whether you are called, gifted, and anointed, to be a minister of the gospel of Jesus Christ, or just one of His kids serving Him in whatever capacity to bring more souls into the family. There is one fact that will never change; No believer is a ministerial asset they are His spiritual offspring, joint heirs with Jesus Christ His Son and partakers in an inheritance of promises and blessings founded upon His eternal plan.

Though we are to minster the gospel to others it is to be by faith upholding our procreative right through natural and supernatural means as revealed by a Spirit of truth written within the scriptures. Truth of all this can be seen in many aspects of the Fathers intentions when He describes Jesus, His first begotten Son.

Luke 3:21-22 Now when all the people were baptized, it came to pass, that Jesus also being baptized, and praying, the heaven was opened, ²² And the Holy Ghost descended in a bodily shape like a dove upon him, and a voice came from heaven, which said, Thou art my beloved Son; in thee I am well pleased.

Jesus was NOT revealed as His ministerial offspring, but as **His beloved Son**, anointed with the Holy Spirit and power to go about doing as God through His work of servitude.

Acts 10:38 (NKJV) how God anointed Jesus of Nazareth with the Holy Spirit and with power, who went about doing good and healing all who were oppressed by the devil, for God was with Him.

Jesus went about delivering all who were oppressed of the devil in His day of ministry. This is because the spiritual DNA in Him is the same as is in His Father making Him an offspring of a Holy God.

The same DNA is in all believers who are brought into the kingdom as offspring of the same God through a sacrifice He made. As we are **spirit** having a soul and living in a body. This fact alone brings to light believers are not to be counted as added assets to the ministerial activity of the Church but as Sons and Daughters of God. And while ministry is to be a focus of all believers it is not an all defining factor for any who know who they are in Christ.

However, it is the work of ministry that defines the Holy Spirit's efforts through us and not solely who we are. Since we are here to be an image of God in this earth done on an individual basis not corporately as seen in ministry. And if the Spirit of God works in those He appoints and anoints then it is inclusive of all who are in Christ and not just a select few who have been deemed the most charismatic of us.

1 Cor 12:4-11 4 Now there are diversities of gifts, but the same Spirit. ⁵ And there are differences of administrations, but the same Lord. ⁶ And there are diversities of operations, but it is <u>the same God which worketh all in all</u>.

These gifts as I mentioned before are for all who are obedient to the Holy Spirit and willing to do His work through them and while they are diverse in activity, all operate solely by supernatural power of God.

However, instead of teaching about gifts and other ministry callings for Him to use according to His will, there is this constant delving into scripture to support doing ministerially outlined works. The following verse is very important for a believer to know, since in it he says the manifestation of the Holy Spirit is given to everyone to <u>profit</u>, but a better translation would be, is to have an advantage.

⁷ But <u>the manifestation of the Spirit is given to every man to profit withal</u>.

An advantage for what? The answer is laid out in scripture for our knowing and understanding that though many have been taught these gifts only operate in those He calls to ministry, or they went away with the disciples or worst yet, they only work in the most holy of Christians. If we let ourselves be taught by the Spirit of God, we find out they are for everyone and that means you, me, and anyone who receives Christ as Lord and savior.

The control of them as to whom and when they operate is under the oversight of the Holy Spirit. And there is nothing here that says He would not use you or me for an operation of them if He sees fit, but we are taught they will only appear as in ministry efforts.

[8] For <u>to one is given by the Spirit</u> the word of wisdom; <u>to another</u> the word of knowledge by the same Spirit; [9] <u>To another faith</u> by the same Spirit; to another the gifts of healing by the same Spirit; [10] <u>To another</u> the working of miracles; <u>to another</u> prophecy; <u>to another</u> discerning of spirits; <u>to another</u> divers kinds of tongues; <u>to another</u> the interpretation of tongues: [11] But <u>all these worketh that one and the selfsame Spirit, dividing to every man severally as he will</u>.

The greatest thing believers can come to know about their life is that they have an *advantage* by the Holy Spirit who works in and through them to do the will of their heavenly Father. This allows Him to bring forth not only gifts within but supernatural gifts for all spiritual purposes He is intent on coming to pass in the world by what we call ministry efforts outlined in the life of Jesus who is our example.

Not everything believers do is a ministerial work in its purpose, our life should be a witness and a testimony that is ongoing whether ministry or plain living. The fact spiritual mediocrity exists reveals taking the most important things an offspring of God should know and make them unknown is by a religious effort.

This has always been supported by ego driven darkness and only makes the Church weaker in spiritual ability. Not one believer is to be used as a ministerial asset without being trained up as a spiritual sibling of God and conscious they are a joint heir with Christ, and in a hierarchical position to be that ministerial asset to the Lord.

It is Jesus the head of the Church who calls believers to any specific ministry of either personal or corporate in His continued efforts of revealing the Father. And every effort to be put forth is to be aligned to the power of God and the authority of His word by the Holy Spirit.

John 14:10-11 *(MSG)* *10 Don't you believe that I am in the Father and the Father is in me? The words that I speak to you aren't mere words. I don't just make them up on my own. The Father who resides in me crafts each word into a divine act.*

If you get nothing else from this book, I pray you get this one truth, words have creative power and in the case of God, it is the very thing that in the beginning the Spirit of God used to bring into existence the whole of creation and continues to transform all who receive by faith His truths.

Genesis 1:3-28 *(MSG)* *3 God spoke: "Light!" And light appeared. 4 God saw that light was good and separated light from dark. 5 God named the light Day, he named the dark Night. It was evening, it was morning— Day One.*

The word God spoke produced light (the Shekinah Glory) and it divided the darkness and the light was called day and the darkness called night.

6 God spoke: "Sky! In the middle of the waters; separate water from water!" 7 God made sky. He separated the water under sky from the water above sky. And there it was: ⁸ he named sky the Heavens; It was evening, it was morning— Day Two.

God's word produced an expanse that appeared between the seas, waters, and oceans and the upper stratosphere to become a breathable atmosphere appearing over the entire earth.

⁹ God spoke: "Separate! Water-beneath-Heaven, gather into one place; Land, appear!" And there it was. ¹⁰ God named the land Earth. He named the pooled water Ocean. God saw that it was good.

His word produced a settling of the waters on the earth and land appeared and divided all the waters we call oceans, seas, rivers, and lakes.

¹¹ God spoke: "Earth, green up! Grow all varieties of seed-bearing plants, Every sort of fruit-bearing tree." And there it was. ¹² Earth produced green seed-bearing plants, all varieties, And fruit-bearing trees of all sorts. God saw that it was good. ¹³ It was evening, it was morning— Day Three.

Every plant, tree, flower, fruit, vegetable, and every green thing we see is for food to eat, and it all came by the word of God. This should tell us how important all of it is to our health and wellbeing of spirit, soul, and body.

¹⁴ God spoke: "Lights! Come out! Shine in Heaven's sky! Separate Day from Night. Mark seasons and days and years, ¹⁵ Lights in Heaven's sky to give light to Earth." And there it was. ¹⁶ God made two big lights, the larger to take charge of Day, The smaller to be in charge of Night; and he made the stars. ¹⁷ God placed them in the heavenly sky to light up Earth ¹⁸ And oversee Day and Night, to separate light and dark. God saw that it was good. ¹⁹ It was evening, it was morning— Day Four.

As much as the glory of the earth alone tells of His majesty, He also made all the heavenly bodies we see and those we still do not.

Then He took a sun and made it ours to light the day and a moon to light the night along with all the stars that remain in the heavens as a guide to those who use them for travel.

20 God spoke: "Swarm, Ocean, with fish and all sea life! Birds, fly through the sky over Earth!" 21 God created the huge whales, all the swarm of life in the waters, And every kind and species of flying birds. God saw that it was good. 22 God blessed them: "Prosper! Reproduce! Fill Ocean! Birds, reproduce on Earth!" 23 It was evening, it was morning— Day Five.

God by His word proclaimed all the life in the oceans and seas and certain living creatures He made in such a way as to be called out, and the birds to have flight over all the earth. Notice He says for them to Prosper, Reproduce, fill the oceans and the birds to also reproduce on earth. Life is in the very essence of His creation and its ability produce more life is according to His word.

24 God spoke: "Earth, generate life! Every sort and kind: cattle and reptiles and wild animals—all kinds." And there it was: 25 wild animals of every kind, Cattle of all kinds, every sort of reptile and bug. God saw that it was good.

Notice He spoke to the earth and said produce life in the form of all cattle, reptiles, and wild beast. This reveals the elements of this planet can produce living creatures. And finally, we see He spoke about humanity, but notice He says we will be the ones to make them, and they will be in our image reflecting our nature. Why? Because humanity is responsible for oversight of all the rest of His creation.

26 God spoke: "Let us make human beings in our image, make them reflecting our nature So they can be responsible for the fish in the sea, the birds in the air, the cattle, And, yes, Earth itself, and every animal that moves on the face of Earth." 27 God created human beings; **_he created them godlike_***, Reflecting God's nature. He*

63

created them male and female. ^{28} God blessed them: "Prosper! Reproduce! Fill Earth! Take charge! Be responsible for fish in the sea and birds in the air, for every living thing that moves on the face of Earth."

Now do not overlook the next important issue here, as to how we are made, in the fact we are to be godlike, as I said before this is not referring to us as gods as He is God, but that we are part of a hierarchy within creation having dominion over all other things.

I pray you see how important it is for you as a child of God to know the truth about who and/or what you are in God's sight. And that through the centuries there has been a religious spirit that blinds God's children from seeing all that He has for them in this life and the one to come.

While ignorance to true ministerial efforts continues to prevail, it is only for a short time more, because God is about to bring it all under judgment in the last days of the Church.

Psalm 37:26-33 *^{26} He is ever merciful, and lendeth; and his seed is blessed. ^{27} Depart from evil, and do good; and dwell for evermore. ^{28} For the LORD loveth judgment, and forsaketh not his saints; they are preserved for ever: but the seed of the wicked shall be cut off. ^{29} The righteous shall inherit the land, and dwell therein forever. ^{30} The mouth of the righteous speaketh wisdom, and his tongue talketh of judgment. ^{31} The law of his God is in his heart; none of his steps shall slide. ^{32} The wicked watcheth the righteous, and seeketh to slay him. ^{33} The LORD will not leave him in his hand, nor condemn him when he is judged.*

God will not leave His sons and daughters to an ignorance that is birthed out of wickedness. What He has said about the righteous is no lie and the judgment that is to come upon those who are filling pulpits and levels of leadership in the churches not doing as He wills has already started.

CHAPTER FOUR

The Spirit of Life

Here is a good place to talk about covenants for a while which are mostly but not always entered in by those in authority or power, since they were often held accountable for the lives of those whom they ruled over. Though they may have been a primary participant of the ceremony the covenant itself often empowered and benefited all persons represented.

As for those who are in covenant with the God of all creation, there must be knowledge and understanding of the sacrifice offered for it. Which as the word of God reveals, is the very life and blood of Jesus the Son of God who came and gave His up, to establish everyone into a covenant with the God who had created them.

John 3:16-17 *For God so loved the world, that he gave his only begotten Son, that whosoever believeth in him should not perish, but have everlasting life. ¹⁷ For* <u>*God sent not his Son into the world to condemn the world;*</u> <u>*but that the world through him might be saved*</u>*.*

The sacrifice Jesus made brought about a New Covenant that we are told is better than the Old Covenant established with God and Abraham.

That covenant required a ceremonial cutting into of animals, and offering of praise, as Abraham passed through them by a lamp.

Gen 15:17 *(GW)* *17 The sun had gone down, and it was dark. Suddenly a smoking oven and a flaming torch passed between the animal pieces.*

In addition to the Abrahamic Covenant was another covenant established upon the Law and given through Moses. This covenant was found not to be possible for Israel to keep in all aspects of a union with God. Requiring something more, so through Jesus a New Covenant was brought into existence.

Heb 8:6-8 *But now hath he obtained a more excellent ministry, by how much also <u>he is the mediator of a better covenant</u>, which was established upon better promises. 7 For if that first covenant had been faultless, then should no place have been sought for the second.*

I want you to notice something in the next verse, the covenant God had established was not the problem, it was Israel and Judah that was the problem, as spiritual mediocrity prevailed in them.

8 For <u>finding fault with them</u>, he saith, Behold, the days come, saith the Lord, when I will make a new covenant with the house of Israel and with the house of Judah.

We will come back to God's covenants with us shortly, but for now I want to spend time on the marriage covenant between a male and female. Starting with a fundamental truth that when entering in marriage each must be willing to engage in a process that is not just some traditional ceremony, but one far more life impacting.

To start with marriage is an ordained process of intercourse that takes place by piercing into each one's life essence to such a degree it can change one's status with God. As the words <u>I DO</u> are uttered by both the male and female there is to be an acceptance of things stating an agreement or covenant is made.

66

Two are making a willful choice to allow their own created life of *spirit, soul,* and *body* be intercourse by the others God created life. The result, two become one in companionship that is built on an eternal promise of God. The essence of this is two lives are now joined for a purpose of fulfilling what we have seen about His creative purpose of males and females.

Each person exists by God's pro-creative power and are *held responsible for their own individual life carried out by their will personally.* Therefore, they must choose whether to give another person the authority, or right, to affect the life they alone are being held accountable for to God.

So, the right or authority for someone to have an influence into one's living existence capable of affecting the outcome they are solely accountable for to God, *requires a covenant type binding or agreement.* I know this is not what you thought was going on when you said I do, but it is the same in the case of your covenant with God through Jesus Christ. You choose whether to give a right and/or an authority for an intercourse of relationship to occur by the Spirit.

The aspect of intercourse here is no different than when Paul talks about sexual unions between husbands and wives, where each has rights to the others flesh, but by authority must give the other a right to engage in sexual intercourse. There is an authority in place in the covenant of marriage regarding both spouses and rights to be an influence upon it must be granted.

1 Cor 7:4-5 [4] *The wife hath not power of her own body, but the husband: and likewise also the husband hath not power of his own body, but the wife.* [5] *Defraud ye not one the other, except it be with consent for a time, that ye may give yourselves to fasting and prayer; and come together again, that Satan tempt you not for your incontinency.*

The Greek word for power is (***exousiazō***) meaning to exercise authority, but the root word is (***exousia***) meaning power or given control of, the sense here is referring to one's flesh and the power or authority given for another person to access it for a purpose of sexual intercourse.

John 1:12 *(AMP) But to as many as did receive and welcome Him, He gave the authority (power, privilege, right) to become the children of God, that is, to those who believe in (adhere to, trust in, and rely on) His name.*

Look at what He says, anyone who receives what my Son has done for them, I give the (***exousia***) right or authority to intercourse into my living existence as My son or daughter, in turn, giving Me the right or authority to intercourse into their life. I used the word intercourse as it best describes the terms of covenant and the type of intimacy these relationships reflect upon us as *spirit*, *soul*, and *body*.

Brightness of Revelation

The fact that you are in such an intimate covenant with God not only has Him as your companion, but Jesus His Son, and the Holy Spirit. Scripture, reveals the making of covenant is defined by a cutting or shedding of blood representative of the essence of life everyone has who enters, so clearly there is more than a ceremonial event going on here. As to be in covenant with God must also have a spiritual intent involved by either the male or female of creation.

Thus, what I believe is being pierced because of these covenants in each person's life, consist of them as *spirit*, or (remnant of God), *soul* (intellect, emotions, feelings, consciousness and will), and the *body* (fleshly house). Is by covenant piercing into the life of another living entity whether it be by the Spirit of God or another person of humanity during the term of covenant.

To understand how important this issue of lives being joined by such an event is, God carved out a 7000-year timeline within His eternal purpose and everything in creation as a part of this timeline manifested when He created the heavens and the earth as described in **Genesis 1: & 2:**

Nothing here is without relevance, He has created males and females in His image and likeness, and empowered them to exercise His spiritual dominion on earth. He operates by faith and has already pre-determined what the end is from the beginning as revealed in His word.

Isa 46:9-10 [9] *Remember the former things of old: for I am God, and there is none else; I am God, and there is none like me;* [10] *Declaring the end from the beginning, and from ancient times things that are not yet done; saying, My counsel shall stand, and I will do all my pleasure;*

When we are born into this timeline at whatever point we enter, we are not in control of it, as to the time, the place, what race, or ethnicity, or social environment was present. But our life influenced by whatever is at work in the world at that time is impacted by what will happen going forward from that point as we live out a fleshly life destined to receive an eternal one.

However, some believe everyone enters at certain or specific times or seasons by God. Though the below scripture does not reveal such aspects, God has predetermined that every one of His creation of males and females, would be His adopted son or daughter through His Son Jesus Christ. Therefore, God is in control of life and death, and everything He has set in motion by the authority and power inherent in His word is to fulfill an eternal purpose.

Eph 1:5 *Having predestinated us unto the adoption of children by Jesus Christ to himself, according to the good pleasure of his will,*

The whole creation represents life on the earth even though death of the flesh will eventually occur. He takes no pleasure in the death of anything in His creation He is a God of life abundant and eternal.

Ezek 18:32 ^(AMP) *For I have no pleasure in the death of him who dies, says the Lord God. Therefore turn (be converted) and live!*

To produce life. Even the dust of the earth can produce life as in **Gen. 1:24**. His covenant that He has entered in with all believers has been done so for the purpose of life both now and eternal.

John 3:16 ^(MSG) *"This is how much God loved the world: He gave his Son, his one and only Son. And this is why: so that no one need be destroyed; by believing in him, <u>anyone can have a whole and lasting life</u>.*

God not only wanted to make an eternal life available, but also make an abundant life available while we are still alive in our fleshly body, living out our part in this timeline. And to ensure an abundant life a covenant is made between God and whomsoever enters it.

John 10:10 ^(AMP) *The thief comes only in order to steal and kill and destroy. I came that they may have and enjoy life, <u>and have it in abundance</u> (to the full, till it overflows).*

Let us talk about the covenant we have with God through Jesus Christ, only Christ's blood was shed for it, making it fundamentally a life purposed covenant, in both a spiritual and natural sense. God is sovereign and perfect in every way, and by supernatural influence He fundamentally changes one's life of *spirit*, *soul*, and *body*, into something to be revealed by a life as He lives.

God in His interaction of covenant is willingly exercising faith at a personal level as God by His Divine nature. Thus, having an influence that if allowed will cut directly into the whole created life of His covenant partners.

Anyone who is a covenant partner, is by faith at their personal level willingly interacting by a new nature within under His grace as who they now are in Christ. All done by a statute of righteousness acceptable to God.

In a like manner husbands and wives in a covenant of marriage are to be actively interacting into each other's lives, cutting into the very life of the other's whole being of *spirit*, *soul*, and *body*, by a nature within that reveal all things are right in the sight of God. If you are married then you know this is true, that each spouse's self-imposed principles founded in their nature has a cutting or piercing affect into the others life.

Another reason the Holy Spirit's revealing of truth for renewed thinking is to transform us, is so we have the same nature at work in us as God does so we will govern ourselves as He does, <u>righteously</u>.

2 Cor 3:18 ^(Darby) *But we all, looking on the glory of the Lord, with unveiled face, are <u>transformed according to the same image from glory to glory</u>, even as by [the] Lord [the] Spirit.*

Whether it be people, events, situations, circumstances, present environment, economic influences, government, and even the social media all these things shape and mold our nature. The things we do seen in our characterization of them is out of our nature based upon these influences.

However, there is to be a fundamental spiritual transformation taking place in every believer due to influences being asserted into their life by the nature of both the creator and the those He created. So, let us not forget this fact, God's covenant is of a spiritual nature as it was established from the beginning of His eternal purpose for all. That means each of us as an individual person is spiritually positioned in the foundation of creation to fulfill a purpose set by God as part of an eternal plan from the beginning.

The family structure is to be the social environment capable of bringing all this about because God has ordained the marriage union before Adam committed treason and before the Church came about. So, there is a specific purpose for marriage beyond procreation that is anointed to create an environment producing life by His seeding processes of both the natural and the supernatural.

There is a revelation to be seen here in that covenant with God promotes a transformation within that ultimately results in an image revealing the divine power and nature of God. Simply put, if a believer works out their salvation in Christ by the Holy Spirit, then through personal covenant with God results of such a process has occurred are revealed. And the eternal purpose He has planned for them as a part of all creation will be exactly what occurs.

Now I want to go back to something I said earlier, an individual in covenant with God is by a work of the Holy Spirit transforming them in nature to do as He does, govern all aspects of themselves as He governs himself. This transformation occurs at the *spiritual level* but influences the whole person's *spirit, soul,* and *body* so every believer must have knowledge and understanding of this activity and be willing to accept the righteous results that occur.

Covet the God Life

Believers are *spirit, soul,* and *body* by God's design, and present in all of them by the Holy Spirit is the very nature of God. This sets the precedence of what is to be the results of such a process as the one we just learned about to bring *spirit* and *soul* growth to maturity.

This is not only to give a believer an ability to see things from a spiritual perspective, but also see there is a choice to do as He does. While there will be those who will not accept such truth, it does not change any spiritual facts about His plan for an eternal life. As all of us must deal with life issues relevant to a social status affecting us in this current era of humanity.

However, for a believer everything must be focused on the truth that shines light on all things pertaining to living by the word of God. Therefore, those who believe in Him are to have a God purposed life originated from the beginning.

Eph 3:11 *According to* <u>*the eternal purpose which he purposed in Christ Jesus our Lord*</u>*:*

God is not forcing anyone to be a part of His great family plan, but He has invited all to be a partaker of it through faith in Jesus Christ His Son. There is nothing in this world that has authority and power over a believer, unless they choose to surrender it to either the enemy who rules in it or someone else.

Remember He said He has spoken all things to us, so that we may have peace in this world. Though we will have tribulation while living in it, we must also be of good cheer because He has already overcome it all for us.

John 16:33 *These things* <u>*I have spoken unto you, that in me ye might have peace*</u>*. In the world ye shall have tribulation: but be of good cheer;* <u>*I have overcome the world*</u>*.*

Now there are those who do not want their loin belt of truth to be full of revelations so for them there is always ignorance. Do not get all wound up, I said this to purposely get your attention, not to insult or offend. But when I make this statement, you will know what I mean as almost everyone has at some point in their life as a believer been led off into a level of spiritual mediocrity which occurs by <u>NOT</u> wanting to do according to the correction of God's word.

Prov 12:1 *(NKJV)* *Whoever loves instruction loves knowledge, But* <u>*he who hates correction is stupid*</u>*.*

If God is our spiritual Father, then we as His spiritual children must commit to His rearing us up in all things as according to the Spirit of God.

Everyone in Christ is to have only one standard they continually apply to their life individually and corporately, and it is the word of God as revealed by the Holy Spirit.

Prov 30:5 *(GW)* "*Every word of God has proven to be true*. He is a shield to those who come to him for protection.*

God's principles are set forth in His word, so that by learning and upholding them we apply truth to a personal and corporate life standard for living, as part of His family heritage. All believers must acquire spiritual sense concerning God and what He is expecting of them regarding a covenant with Him, this means they must keep all truths in their heart as revealed in scripture.

Prov 4:20-23 *20 My son, attend to my words; incline thine ear unto my sayings. 21 Let them not depart from thine eyes; keep them in the midst of thine heart.*

Here is something we must do daily, nurture our *soul* and *spirit* and our children's so all are spiritually conscious of instructions by the Holy Spirit.

22 For they are life unto those that find them, and health to all their flesh. 23 Keep thy heart with all diligence; for out of it are the issues of life.

If God fails to nurture those who are possessors of a spirit life, He gave them, how could He receive the true fellowship from them as revealed in His word. Everything we have seen so far is to reveal we are to be free as children of God in relationship with the Lord to receive the counsel and instruction of the Spirit of Life.

Knowing there is coming an event where everyone will give an account reveals many today have problems with being accountable for doing things regarding the spiritual aspects of God. Since they want to take a more passive role, mainly because they are not sure of what they need to know.

Rom 14:12 So then <u>every one of us shall give account of himself to God</u>.

I believe the Holy Spirit's role is much more than we know, and we will only come to the place of discerning all things as we take responsibility for who we are in relationship with Him. The darkness of the curse that came upon all creation at the fall no longer has a hold on those who receive the truth and are willing to take their rightful place as part of a royal family whose heritage is founded upon righteousness.

This revelation along with many others have been purposely kept hidden by the religious and pious leaders of most of the Church for centuries. Thus, it is no wonder we are spiritually ineffective and mediocre at best in the aspect of supernatural power.

1 Peter 2:9 *⁹ But ye are a chosen generation, a royal priesthood, an holy nation, a peculiar people; that ye should shew forth the praises of him who hath called you out of darkness into his marvelous light:*

However, those who receive Christ as Lord and savior, and take God at His word will take their place in a hierarchical position of spiritual responsibility while working out salvation as His offspring. This requires an exercising of faith that can only increase by the word of God, not by applying the ways of the world.

Rom 1:17 *(AMP) For in the Gospel a righteousness which God ascribes is revealed, both springing from faith and leading to faith [disclosed through the way of faith that arouses to more faith]. As it is written, The man who through faith is just and upright shall live and shall live by faith.*

It is the devil who is the one truly committed to keeping not only believers ignorant and spiritually stupid regarding a position in the family of God, but all of creation.

Responsibility as part of God's plan is each actively applying things to be seen through them, so by a life changing covenant all aspects of their created being of *spirit*, *soul,* and *body* is fulfilled. Believers are responsible to fulfill God's expectations as males and females of His creation, a spiritual heritage. And it is not something that will be done by Him, or the Lord Jesus Christ, or the Holy Spirit, only by those who by covenant of truth fulfill His eternal purpose.

So, what you need to know is that included in this heritage is a willingness to fulfill a procreative process to bring forth offspring both naturally and supernaturally. This requires environments like families and churches, where He can spiritually nurture the core of every believer He is committed to, and does it for all who enter.

2 Cor 4:1-7 [1] Therefore seeing we have this ministry, as we have received mercy, we faint not; [2] But have renounced the hidden things of dishonesty, not walking in craftiness, nor handling the word of God deceitfully; but <u>by manifestation of the truth commending ourselves to every man's conscience in the sight of God</u>.

Paul in response to the people's assumption there may be some manner of deceit in the gospel they preach to them makes it clear he and those with him reject all dishonesty and deceit. He is adamite that what they preach is the truth and nothing but the truth.

[3] But if our gospel be hid, it is hid to them that are lost: [4] In whom the god of this world hath blinded the minds of them which believe not, lest the light of the glorious gospel of Christ, who is the image of God, should shine unto them.

Those who are lost have no life from which they can live the truth but continue to remain in darkness until an image of the gospel is manifested by the light of revelation through the work of the Spirit of God. Which reveals a blood covenant with Him through Christ is available.

⁵ For we preach not ourselves, but Christ Jesus the Lord; and ourselves your servants for Jesus' sake. ⁶ For God, who commanded the light to shine out of darkness, hath shined in our hearts, to give the light of the knowledge of the glory of God in the face of Jesus Christ. ⁷ But we have this treasure in earthen vessels, that the excellency of the power may be of God, and not of us.

Believers cannot deny what God is doing in and through them is to bring the whole body to the maturity needed to faithfully stand as the spirit of life offspring He declares we are.

This is so the power to be manifested through us is clearly seen by those lost in sin. Thus, the covenant we have with the God who has created all things is by far and away more valuable than we know and makes understanding how to avoid spiritual mediocrity in this day and hour a paramount issue.

The Law of The Spirit of Life

Rom 8:2 ² For the law of the <u>Spirit of life in Christ Jesus</u> hath made me free from the law of sin and death.

While we have seen a covenant with God through Christ is one of life there is a law associated to this, and it is a law that has not only given us this spirit of life but more importantly has set us free from sin and death.

Once we accept Christ as our Lord and savior this law is applied to us setting us free from the law that bound us to sin and eternal death. Job understood he was a creation of God and the very life that flowed in his body was the life essence of God himself.

Job 33:4 ⁴ The Spirit of God hath made me, and the breath of the Almighty hath given me life.

The main event in Job's life when Satan was given access to trial him and try to get him to curse God, was all focused upon his physical life.

God told Satan he could trial him by removing all his blessings and bring affliction upon his flesh, but he could not kill him. Why? Because Job feared God, and though he made mistakes he believed in God. Jesus had not died in Job's time but His sacrifice for a spirit of life from God to be in us as He determined in the creation was accounted to Job's right standing.

Job 42:12-17 *[12] So the LORD blessed the latter end of Job more than his beginning: for he had fourteen thousand sheep, and six thousand camels, and a thousand yoke of oxen, and a thousand she asses. [13] He had also seven sons and three daughters. [14] And he called the name of the first, Jemima; and the name of the second, Kezia; and the name of the third, Kerenhappuch. [15] And in all the land were no women found so fair as the daughters of Job: and their father gave them inheritance among their brethren.*

In the end Job came out blessed more than when he was brought into the tribulation. God proved He is not into death and destruction as some would like us to believe. And though He destroys for the sake of righteousness, He as a sovereign God has the right to.

[16] After this lived Job an hundred and forty years, and saw his sons, and his sons' sons, even four generations. [17] So Job died, being old and full of days.

Since in every aspect of our life God is revealed to us as one who shows an eternal life, a heritage through covenant with God is based upon righteousness. If you understand the righteousness you have in Christ it should remove from you all spiritual mediocrity, since to know who you are in Him is to know who God says you are before Him. Therefore, we are established as living spirits holding a statute of right standing before Him through Jesus Christ our Lord.

Rom 8:10 *[10] And if Christ be in you, the body is dead because of sin; but the Spirit is life because of righteousness.*

I cannot express enough how far the body of Christ is removed from knowing who they are because of leadership fearful of the truth that brings forth exactly what they know will occur. Spiritually alive offspring who know and understand the intent and concern in the heart of their Father God and know whom they are in Christ Jesus.

2 Cor 3:17-18 *¹⁷ Now <u>the Lord is that Spirit</u>: and <u>where the Spirit of the Lord is</u>, <u>there is liberty</u>. ¹⁸ <u>But we all</u>, with open face beholding as in a glass the glory of the Lord, <u>are changed into the same image from glory to glory</u>, <u>even as by the Spirit of the Lord</u>.*

Living under the law of the spirit of life free from the law of sin and death means a believer's liberty from sin and death in Christ releases them to behold the glory of the Lord and be changed into the same image from glory to glory.

Look closely at what he says next, *even as by the Spirit of the Lord*. We are to be by the Spirit as He was on this earth. I know many are thinking but I am not Christ, true but you are joint heirs and siblings made in the flesh and re-gene-rated in the spirit to be as He is.

Phil 3:8-9 *(MSG)* *⁸ Yes, all the things I once thought were so important are gone from my life. Compared to the high privilege of knowing Christ Jesus as my Master, firsthand, everything I once thought I had going for me is insignificant—dog dung. I've dumped it all in the trash so that I could embrace Christ ⁹ and be embraced by him. I didn't want some petty, <u>inferior brand of righteousness</u> that comes from keeping a list of rules when I could get the robust kind that comes from trusting Christ—<u>God's righteousness</u>.*

Paul's implication of receiving righteousness reveals to us we are to give up all things we have gained for the sake of right standing religious leaders say we only have by works. So, let us finish this with learning something else Paul wrote to Christians in Rome about in how all have been brought under the work of Christ sacrifice.

Rom 3:19-26 *(MSG)* *19 This makes it clear, doesn't it, that whatever is written in these Scriptures is not what God says about others but to us to whom these Scriptures were addressed in the first place! And it's clear enough, isn't it, that we're sinners, every one of us, in the same sinking boat with everybody else?*

He is explaining the statute of sinner before God is accounted to all who are a part of the creation. Though he and everyone with him and even us are complicit in the aspects of sin, something new has been added to the equation.

It is a testimony that has come from those of the past who gave witness to a time when God would settle all things with humanity having to do with sin. And clearly from these verses it is Jesus who is the one who settled the account of sin.

20 Our involvement with God's revelation doesn't put us right with God. What it does is force us to face our complicity in everyone else's sin. 21 But in our time something new has been added. What Moses and the prophets witnessed to all those years has happened. 22 The God-setting-things-right that we read about has become Jesus-setting-things-right for us. And not only for us, but for everyone who believes in him. For there is no difference between us and them in this.

The spirit of life you and I have exists because we are in a right standing with God our Heavenly Father, not through anything we have done but through what Jesus has done for us. There is nothing a believer can ever do that will equal what He has done because it is spiritual and empowered by supernatural ability.

23 Since we've compiled this long and sorry record as sinners (both us and them) and proved that we are utterly incapable of living the glorious lives God wills for us, 24 God did it for us. Out of sheer generosity he put us in right standing with himself. A pure gift. He got us out of the mess we're in and restored us to where he always wanted us to be. And he did it by means of Jesus Christ. ²⁵ God sacrificed Jesus on the altar of the world to clear that world of sin.

Having faith in Him sets us free from the curse and moves us out into the clear openness of freedom to be who we are to be in the sight of God and to live the spirit of life He wills for us.

Having faith in him sets us in the clear. God decided on this course of action in full view of the public—to set the world in the clear with himself through the sacrifice of Jesus, finally taking care of the sins he had so patiently endured. ²⁶ This is not only clear, but it's now—this is current history! God sets things right. He also makes it possible for us to live in his rightness.

Amazing what He says in the previous verse in that it is current history proving out it is possible for us to live in His righteousness. How important is that? A believer able to live in the rightness of God, is in contrast with several theological text I know about that iterate once a sinner always a sinner.

I remember way back in my early days in Christ as I sat fixated on every word that came out of the mouth of whoever was behind the pulpit putting forth teachings and/or exhortations from scripture. Many of which I adhere to even today though my knowledge and understanding might go beyond what was revealed then. Fact is truth cannot contradict truth. But at that time, I knew nothing about the power of the covenant with God or the creative power of His word, nor how to live by the word and the Spirit of life.

Psalm 119:169-172 ¹⁶⁹ Let my cry come near before thee, O LORD: give me understanding according to thy word. ¹⁷⁰ Let my supplication come before thee: deliver me according to thy word. ¹⁷¹ My lips shall utter praise, when thou hast taught me thy statutes. ¹⁷² My tongue shall speak of thy word: for all thy commandments are righteousness.

The freedom we saw earlier allows believers the opportunity to make a personal decision to live according to what He has said about them, and not what the law of sin and death says. As there are no believers who are perfected in all of this because there are no perfect people, however, there is the word that leads to perfection of love and grace by the Spirit.

Every believer is offered the same opportunity of life in Christ which is an abundance of it founded upon the sacrifices He made to redeem them from the curse of the law of sin and death. Anyone who counters this truth is without fear of who God is and what He does or has done in the light of truth.

Gal 3:11-14 ¹¹ But that no man is justified by the law in the sight of God, it is evident: for, The just shall live by faith. ¹² And the law is not of faith: but, The man that doeth them shall live in them. ¹³ Christ hath redeemed us from the curse of the law, being made a curse for us: for it is written, Cursed is every one that hangeth on a tree:

The blessings of Abraham are still working today in the lives of all who by faith are redeemed from the curse of the law and made justified by Christ sacrifice.

¹⁴ That the blessing of Abraham might come on the Gentiles through Jesus Christ; that we might receive the promise of the Spirit through faith.

It is important believers remember though Christ has redeemed them from such a curse, it is freedom from condemnation that bolds His purpose on their behalf.

Rom 8:1 ¹ There is therefore now no condemnation to them which are in Christ Jesus, who walk not after the flesh, but after the Spirit.

The whole aspect of the Spirit of life is so every believer can live in the total freedom He has provided for them. Churches and pulpits who render a worldly perspective more than a Godly one is not in light to the truth revealed in scripture but fixated upon the social dialog of the day that speaks of a way of death more than life.

John 5:24 *24 Verily, verily, I say unto you, He that heareth my word, and believeth on him that sent me, <u>hath everlasting life</u>, and <u>shall not come into condemnation</u>; but is <u>passed from death unto</u> <u>life</u>.*

It is never going to be God's will for your living a life that is more in tune to the death of both flesh and spirit as is detailed in the curse. And nothing about a believer's presence here is associated to death as they were before they believed in Jesus Christ. Since they are now in a state of everlasting life free from hell. Death, and the grave.

1 Cor 15:51-57 *51 Behold, <u>I shew you a mystery</u>; We shall not all sleep, but we shall all be changed, 52 In a moment, in the twinkling of an eye, at the last trump: for the trumpet shall sound, and the dead shall be raised incorruptible, and we shall be changed.*

This is not a mystery, you if you have Christ as your Lord, are in the sight of God as one having eternal or everlasting life and death is no longer seen as a part of you. The reason I say it is not a mystery is because it is now revealed by the truth of the word and the Spirit of God no longer hidden from believers and their right to know such truth.

53 For this corruptible must put on incorruption, and this mortal must put on immortality. 54 So when this corruptible shall have put on incorruption, and this mortal shall have put on immortality, then shall be brought to pass the saying that is written, <u>Death is</u> <u>swallowed up in victory</u>. 55 <u>O death, where is thy sting</u>? <u>O grave,</u> <u>where is thy victory</u>?

While death of one's flesh may still occur, it is not the final act of the curse that came upon all humanity at Adams fall, Christ has victory over death and the result of His death and resurrection is now accounted to all who believe. It is a part of the covenant you have with God through Jesus Christ His Son, that speaks of your eternal promise made to you before you were ever born.

56 The sting of death is sin; and the strength of sin is the law. 57 But thanks be to God, which giveth us the victory through our Lord Jesus Christ.

CHAPTER FIVE

Dominion vs Domination

The aspect of you as a part of creation having dominion on earth has always been an underlying issue for believers, but among most churches of today it is a taboo subject, as pulpits are fearful it might promote a sense of power. It is about power but a power the Holy Spirit wants to teach us by explanation of how spiritual principles reveal such power from the word of God.

If we look at the Church and God's purpose for it, we see it is here to represent the standards of His kingdom while manifesting a righteous life, having His power and authority prevailing. But most believers are struggling to just live righteously, often because they are doing it using worldly principles or applying religious ideals that have created apostate mannerisms of living. And there is evidence not all church members are of a mind to live by kingdom standards, as is seen by the world through today's overbearing social activism.

This occurs when consciousness to the eternal things of God is not yet developed in a believer's spirit due to doctrines that are overly appropriated and designed to maintain a more infantile state of spiritual growth in its occupants, as seen from pulpits of today.

Whether unconscious or just infantile it is maintained by an ill-purposed doctrine, what is revealed in the 66 books we call our modern bible is every believer has a righteous standing in God. And no one in the body of Christ is perfect or let us just say fully matured spiritually and living for God as they truly could be by the word.

The only one whoever revealed such a maturity is Jesus, but He reveals to us that we can live a life in the flesh while manifesting the very nature of our Father God.

The Church of today is to be growing as a corporate body made up of all its individual parts, each created by God to spiritually grow and mature by truths revealed in His word. Do not let the fact that we are not yet there stop any of us in our spiritual tracks, we have all been redeemed *spirit, soul,* and *body* through the work of Jesus Christ, giving us free access to all truths.

These are truths we need to view as one having spiritual sense, especially as the body of Christ, since it is made up of born-again believers supernaturally set apart from this world to be His righteous representatives of this dominion.

However, as I said the reality is most of the Church struggles in its attempt to manifest itself as such a body, since many are living by worldly and religious mannerisms having a spiritual mediocrity to a righteous standard.

Think of it this way, Jesus the spiritual head of the Church is by a Divine nature working through the Holy Spirit to manifest the will of His Father into this earth and yet He is doing it with a body that has a spiritual nature immature of truth.

1 Cor 12:12-13 *(NKJV)* *For as the body is one and has many members, but all the members of that one body, being many, are one body, so also is Christ.*

Thus, it is time to open our minds and hearts to allow the Holy Spirit to reveal truths regarding the Church and this dominion God has said is to be present here, which is clearly revealed as part of our heritage as sons and daughters of God.

To start with the Church is not a building or denomination or a religious group, it is those who are called as one body having many parts baptized into one Spirit all growing as matured offspring, by the Spirit and the word. But it has been divided by those who see it as a platform for enforcing a domination of power and authority not in alignment to this individual and corporate dominion.

¹³ For by one Spirit we were all baptized into one body--whether Jews or Greeks, whether slaves or free--and have all been made to drink into one Spirit.

What we find out is that all believers are not being matured to the same level or by the same spirit to a renewed thinking showing something is wrong, or God clearly misstated the way we are to be. But I am pretty sure it is the former not the later that is the problem.

Rom 12:2 *And be not conformed to this world: but be ye transformed by the renewing of your mind, that ye may prove what is that good, and acceptable, and perfect, will of God.*

There are parts of the Church who once stood in the pews and revealed a manner of living reflecting a new life in Christ, but over time they have slid away from any righteous ways back to more worldly ones. They typically are still being counted as part of the body but separated in a spiritual sense from the whole, lacking in truths. These are the ones we call backsliders, who once stood at the altar, but are now missing in action.

Prov 14:14 *The backslider in heart shall be filled with his own ways: and a good man shall be satisfied from himself.*

There are other parts who confess Jesus as Lord and for a while are counted as believers, but if remain infant because of milk and no mature meat of the word they struggle to have senses learned to the truth and often enter despair over no teaching of any knowledge of a life in Christ.

Heb 5:13-14 For <u>everyone that useth milk is unskilful in the word of righteousness</u>: for he is a babe. ¹⁴ But strong meat belongeth to them that are of full age, even those who by reason of use have their senses exercised to discern both good and evil.

Then there are the new converts who just received a new birth in Christ and are unlearned in everything. And what about all those unbelievers who enter among the sheep to find comfort? Where do they fit into all of this?

1 Cor 14:23-25 If therefore the whole church be come together into one place, and all speak with tongues, and <u>there come in those that are unlearned, or unbelievers</u>, will they not say that ye are mad?

Finally, we have those who occupy a seat in the assembly, but are so worldly minded they are unwilling to be transformed by the Spirit of God. Live according to the world's way and interpret truths of the word through carnal intellect relying upon traditions and customs of men to support their position. I call these individuals the *spiritually stupid*, as they always despise correction and unwilling to be transformed by scriptural truth.

Prov 12:1 ^(NKJV) ¹ Whoever loves instruction loves knowledge, But <u>he who hates correction is stupid</u>.

Throughout the Church's history denominations and religious sects have been so dominate over what believers are taught many live as immature in their level of spiritual growth in the body. True there are some who grew despite levels of spiritual density among leadership, but most have not grown as God would see them.

Many denominational based church goers often reveal some spiritual ignorance in times of tribulation and inherently are in a danger of doing whatever is said by the world, when the fact is it is really being said about Christ.

As for me as a part of Christ body, I am at my level of spiritual maturity because of my willingness to be taught the word of God by the Holy Spirit. No one is forcing me to do this, not God or my Lord Jesus Christ, or even the Holy Spirit himself, because they respect my will. But since it is my will to grow and since God has already done all things for it to happen, I can receive the blessing of spiritual growth by the word. And no, I am not perfect or fully matured at this moment, but neither is anybody else in the body of Christ for that matter.

Full spiritual maturity according to the word does not occur until one enters His presence, until then we will require continued revelation. The reality is, believers have no excuse not to grow spiritually, and take their place as God's child, and since no one else on earth is qualified to do such a thing He makes it appear as if a commandment.

2 Tim 2:20-21 (NKJV) *But in a great house there are not only vessels of gold and silver, but also of wood and clay, some for honor and some for dishonor.* [21] *Therefore <u>if anyone cleanses himself from the latter, he will be a vessel for honor, sanctified and useful for the Master, prepared for every good work</u>.*

I know it does not say I command you, but nothing here excuses us from our responsibility as a child of God, rather it enforces what is clear from scripture that He has an expectation of all to personally take account of themselves. In case you did not know none of this is about believers anyway, it always was, always is, and always will be about Jesus and Him crucified and the Church's revealing of it.

So, how does spiritual maturity fit into this aspect of dominion vs domination? Well as we already saw, it is God's will that we as a part of His family be spiritually mature and able to operate in an authority and power that ensure things occur for the wellbeing of all its parts.

What is wellbeing? In its general term it means a state reflecting the *quality of life of an individual, or the whole being of a person.* Quality of life is typically measured by one's physical health (*body*) and or mental health (*soul*), with a spiritual perspective not usually acknowledged, but generally considered an influence. This is how the world measures quality of life or the wellbeing of an individual, or group, or even a nation.

1 Pet 1:23 Being born again, not of corruptible seed, but <u>of incorruptible, by the word of God</u>, which liveth and abideth forever.

We are born in the natural, and then born again in the spirit from an eternal spiritual seed, it is a seed that is incorruptible producing a *living spirit* by a process that has no accommodation for mediocrity.

Since such a state only lends to a servitude metered out under a guise of religious and/or denominational terms. Believers must know they are no longer spiritually dead as they were before coming to Christ. And there is now a requirement from God considering one's wellbeing as measured by the healthiness of their *spirit*. This means *spiritual maturity* must be considered, and effort by pulpits made to provide truths for it to occur.

A Living Entity

This effort of spiritual health is something we will see requires the orchestrator of it be the Holy Spirit since those things that bring maturity and stability for believers, their family, and the Church are all within the confines of the word of God.

Mal 2:15 *(MSG)* *GOD, not you, made marriage. His Spirit inhabits even the smallest details of marriage. And what does he want from marriage?* <u>*Children of God*</u>*, that's what. So guard the spirit of marriage within you. Don't cheat on your spouse.*

This verse gives testimony to marriage from when God said He has an eternal purpose employed for it by a process, He perceived would bring about His spiritual offspring. Thus, any who enter in a marriage covenant influenced by the Spirit of God are seen as being righteous provisioners.

1 John 3:7 *(AMP)* *Boys (lads), let no one deceive and lead you astray.* <u>*He who practices righteousness*</u> *[who is upright, conforming to the divine will in purpose, thought, and action, living a consistently conscientious life]* <u>*is righteous*</u>*,* <u>*even as He is righteous*</u>*.*

The Church filled with those living in such a manner, is filled with the peace of God, resting on the factual truth all are in covenant with the creator, and fully conscious of who they are in Christ Jesus. These same believers will not allow themselves to be persuaded by religiously formatted doctrines to live as the world does, but will by faith in the Son of God, corporately rely on His power and authority.

I told you the enemy wants to keep all of us spiritually ignorant, so we cannot operate at a level God decreed from the beginning. Most see spiritual maturity as having knowledgeable understanding of God and His word through our relationship with Christ. And rely on ministry gifts of Pastor, Teacher, Evangelist, Apostle and Prophet along with the Holy Spirit, to help them learn.

While these things are true in respect to all God is doing, it is not all the truth regarding a created ability to mature as offspring. Spiritual growth comes by faith in a progressive process that is illustrated throughout the word of God purposed to take one from *infancy* to *maturity*. We can compare this to human natural growth where every male or female born into the earth has a growth process.

One that is built into their DNA that affects both physical and mental aspects as they mature. As such it is God's designed process that ensure a level of maturity is reached as a part of His created humanity. Thus, we have ability to grow up spiritually to a level of maturity.

Eph 4:13-14 *(NKJV) till we all come to the unity of the faith and of the knowledge of the Son of God, to a perfect man, to the measure of the stature of the fullness of Christ; That <u>we henceforth be no more children</u>, tossed to and fro, and carried about with every wind of doctrine, by the sleight of men, and cunning craftiness, whereby they lie in wait to deceive.*

This is not something we are able fulfill on our own, it requires someone who already has such spiritual maturity present. Therefore, Christ sent the Holy Spirit to be that someone revealing to us what we need to know so we grow in each level of this process.

Unlike an orphan who is without parents or legal guardian to take responsibility for them, we have a heritage and lineage. Praise God, He is not an irresponsible parent who will leave His offspring helpless and unable to cope with life and struggling with worldly influence by a killer enemy.

The word in the following verse for comfortless is (***orphanos***) meaning one who is fatherless or an orphan, it is someone Jesus says believers are not going to be.

John 14:18 *I will not leave you <u>comfortless</u>: I will come to you.*

Now considering all the denominations that exist in the Church today ask yourself; Do all believers know who they truly are as a child of God? If so, then why do many of them appear immature and ignorant of that truth? I do not ask to make anyone feel bad but to have you reflect on why believers are so different in their faith and all over the place in spiritual knowledge and understanding.

Is it possible all the doctrines and by-laws and piously religious rules have not been able to do what the word says only happens by truth contained within and the work of Holy Spirit?

Math 16:15-17 He saith unto them, But whom say ye that I am? ¹⁶ And Simon Peter answered and said, Thou art the Christ, the Son of the living God. ¹⁷ And Jesus answered and said unto him, Blessed art thou, Simon Barjona: for flesh and blood hath not revealed it unto thee, but my Father which is in heaven.)

The Spirit of God is not under any organizational rules or by-laws, He operates solely by the will of God and any revealing of truth He brings forth is purposely occurring.

Jesus explained when God revealed to Peter, that by revelation truth is now uncovered or unveiled by the Spirit to him. He called it a revealing that came solely by His heavenly Father. This process is to continually move believers further away from their old carnal nature, to a more Divine and spiritually mature one.

1 Cor. 13:11-12 (AMP) When I was a child, I talked like a child, I thought like a child, I reasoned like a child; now that I have become a man, I am done with childish ways and have put them aside. ¹² For now we are looking in a mirror that gives only a dim (blurred) (spiritual) reflection [of reality as in a riddle or enigma], but then [when perfection comes] we shall see in reality and face to face! Now I know in part (imperfectly), but then I shall know and understand fully and clearly, even in the same manner as I have been fully and clearly known and understood [by God].

Paul says in the natural one grows up from childhood to adult, in the same manner we will also grow up spiritually, even though right now spiritual things seem cloudy, dim, and partly revealed. But there will come a time when such things become clearly known and understood, as we are clearly and fully known by God. And much of it will occur while we are still in our fleshly bodies.

Our spiritual and physical growth was to be automatic because it was genetically wired into a biological codex at creation, and the DNA in that biological codex influences or controls a perceived outcome just as our Heavenly Father determined. Unfortunately, the spiritual part of this process was put in a dormant state as result of sin present in Adam that flowed through all of humanity. A result of one man's offence as the word says.

Rom. 5:12 *(AMP)* *Therefore, as <u>sin came into the world through one man</u>, and death as the result of sin, so death spread to all men, [no one being able to stop it or to escape its power] <u>because all men sinned</u>.*

God's DNA which contains this spiritual codex cannot die, and it is in us, it is the *spirit* life that came from Him in the beginning. Adam who represented humanity was created to be the first of an eternal lineage living throughout eternity with God.

Gen 2:7 *(AMP)* *Then the Lord God formed man from the dust of the ground and <u>breathed into his nostrils the breath or spirit of life</u>, and <u>man became a living being</u>.*

Not only does the process that creates a ***born-again*** believer make a spirit alive in doing so it re-starts this spiritual process of growth, so they will grow into the whole being as purposed. Those who rightfully are born of the *spirit* of God require a life-giving connection be present by the Holy Spirit to be fully alive which can only occur through faith in Christ.

As stated, the nature to sin entered Adam, disconnecting him and us from that spiritually completed maturity we are destined to have. But when we become a new creation in Christ, God's DNA or spiritual codex has been re-activated or as the word says re-gene-rated by the Holy Spirit. Thus, the growth process He determined to occur in us starts again just as He purposed it to be because *we* are the only part of creation that by the word produces *spirit* life.

You are not just created by the word but for the word to fulfill an eternal plan. Angels on the other hand are created as spiritual beings living in heaven and on earth, they are created for heavenly purposes, you were created for earthly purposes. They are spirits who minister to all who come to be made righteous through Christ salvation, so every believer has these ministering spirits about them to command.

Heb 1:14 *(NKJV)* *Are they not all ministering spirits sent forth to minister for those who will inherit salvation?*

God is leaving no one out of this process, as every genetically correct male and female of humanity have been created with the ability to become His spiritual offspring who are to be rulers over His earthly creation *Ps 8:4-9*.

Whatever position each may be called to in Christ, it requires a certain level of spiritual maturity be brought by the word of God by the Holy Spirit to be accomplished so that this dominion status is fulfilled.

Believers reveal God through Christ and is why the Church is to be a spiritual incubator, so all who come into it are provided a controlled environment for an individual growth in spirit to occur.

Mark 16:15-17 *(AMP)* *And He said to them, Go into all the world and preach and publish openly the good news (the Gospel) to every creature [of the whole human race].* *16 He who believes [who adheres to and trusts in and relies on the Gospel and Him Whom it sets forth] and is baptized will be saved [from the penalty of eternal death]; but he who does not believe [who does not adhere to and trust in and rely on the Gospel and Him Whom it sets forth] will be condemned.* *17 And these attesting signs will accompany those who believe: in My name they will drive out demons; they will speak in new languages;*

Since our responsibility is to fulfill works of servitude it reveals the gospel of Christ and His work on the cross is for those who have not an image of God seen in them. Christ requires a body capable of manifesting spiritual gifts, signs, wonders, and miracles on the earth.

This requires an ability to present everything that reveals truth about who God is as a heavenly Father who created us. The fact this is not occurring throughout the body of Christ reveals that doctrines exists for expressing biased ministry.

Eph 2:8-9 *(NKJV)* *For by grace you have been saved through faith, and that not of yourselves; it is the gift of God, [9] not of works, lest anyone should boast.*

Another important fact to remember is, that God has not made any believer His ministering son or daughter most especially by any denominationally religious event. But, by love through grace enacts a salvation plan that cost the life of His precious Son to make them His spiritual offspring.

It is important to know, it is not now, nor has it ever been, about ministry or ones sacrifice within it. It is and always will be about obedience to the truths revealed by the Holy Spirit for the maturity of all His offspring.

1 Sam15:22 *(MSG)* *Then Samuel said, Do you think all GOD wants are sacrifices— empty rituals just for show? He wants you to listen to him! Plain listening is the thing, not staging a lavish religious production.*

Since the Holy Spirit is responsible for all truths to be known by the family of God those who are His offspring have been given responsibility to have supernatural ability to operate in this earth in obedience to them. Having knowledge and understanding of who they are so a dominion on the earth occurs according to His purposed plan.

The Church is here for only one purpose, to reconcile the world to God through Jesus Christ His Son. Which is revealed by works of servitude accompanied with signs, wonders, and miracles, revealed beforehand in the truth of the word. Not to sustain some variance of faith sown for the purpose of holding up denominations that lean not to the truth that all are equal as sons and daughters or testifying of a dominion purposed by God.

What every believer must learn by the Holy Spirit is, Jesus the Son of God is the one who has spiritually positioned them to have supernatural authority capable of fulfilling the Fathers eternal plan. This cannot be changed in this present age or in the age to come, it is founded upon Christ who is the beginning and end of all things, the Alpha, and the Omega.

Rev 1:8 *I am Alpha and Omega, the beginning and the ending, saith the Lord, which is, and which was, and which is to come, the Almighty.*

For an everlasting dominion to operate through Jesus's body of believers they must obtain a level of spiritual maturity that equips them to have a manner of fortitude enabling all to perceive every truth for the same eternal purpose.

Dan 7:14 *(AMP)* *And there was given Him [the Messiah] dominion and glory and kingdom, that all peoples, nations, and languages should serve Him. His dominion is an everlasting dominion which shall not pass away, and His kingdom is one which shall not be destroyed.*

The works Christ has done is for everyone, so no believer needs to focus on why they are here, and what Jesus desires for them to do, but in their servitude to the Father do His will. And they will fulfill a place in His plan of salvation having dominion and authority that reveals in their witness and testimony a level of maturity, that does not appear by any domination or its doctrines.

The unfolding of truth that reveals why this dominion must be present presents the body of Christ with another situation this one concerns our acceptance of one another. As divided assemblies we have over many decades rejected our diversity and stood proudly on denominational platforms biasedly upholding our right to be who leadership says we are.

Eph 4:1-3 *(GW)* *I, a prisoner in the Lord, encourage you to live the kind of life which proves that God has called you.* *²* *Be humble and gentle in every way. Be* <u>*patient with each other and lovingly*</u> <u>*accept each other.*</u> *³* *Through the peace that ties you together, do your best to maintain the unity that the Spirit gives.*

If there is to be any harmony and unity among God's siblings, then enforcing it must be by expressing certain aspects that reveal humility, gentleness, patience, Agape - love, and accepting of one another. And working to maintain a *unity of spiritual fellowship* by the Holy Spirit, that can only come by a maturity each has available in Jesus Christ.

Since every believer has been supernaturally seated in Christ with authority and power, they are by a heavenly presence seated together to occupy with him and the Father. And as mentioned already, evidence of you being a child of God is you working out your salvation with fear and trembling in respect of, the authority and power of God.

Eph 2:6 *And hath raised us up together, and* <u>*made us sit*</u> <u>*together in heavenly places in Christ Jesus:*</u>

Jesus is at the right hand of the Father, and daily He intercedes on our behalf continually ensuring our presence through grace as the family of God. However, spiritual mediocrity in those who accept doctrines of men leaves gaps in our fellowship that can only be filled through communion by the Holy Spirit.

Rom 8:34 ^(AMP) *Who is there to condemn [us]? Will Christ Jesus (the Messiah), Who died, or rather Who was raised from the dead, Who is at the right hand of God actually pleading as He intercedes for us?*

It was Jesus Christ who made us God's sons and daughters, to be equipped and matured. Thus, the reconciliation of humanity is not to be taken lightly as it has eternal ramifications, and it occurs both in and out of the Church. But true Christianity is to live life revealing a personal relationship with the Father and the Son is by the Holy Spirit's working in and through each in unity.

Phil 2:12-15 Wherefore, my beloved, as ye have always obeyed, not as in my presence only, but now much more in my absence, <u>work out your own salvation with fear and trembling</u>. ¹³ For it is God which worketh in you both to will and to do of his good pleasure. ¹⁴ Do all things without murmurings and disputings: ¹⁵ That ye may be blameless and harmless, <u>the sons of God</u>, without rebuke, in the midst of a crooked and perverse nation, among whom ye shine as lights in the world;

Believers are employed to do God's will by their own personal experience of deliverance as His son or daughter. Conscious of the heavenly Father's intent and concern regarding their spiritual life and His will to be revealed through it, and the salvation of those yet to enter in. This is all revealed in Jesus's humility, where-by His sustaining, prophetic foundations based on God's doctrine contrived by the Holy Spirit, was not by those who desire to control truths about Him. You are in the form of God, which is by *spirit* and *soul,* or likeness and image, meaning you are not to think it robbery to be equal with Him.

Phil 2:5-11 Let this mind be in you, which was also in Christ Jesus: ⁶ Who, <u>being in the form of God</u>, thought it <u>not robbery to be equal with God</u>:

You willing to take on a form of a servant in humbling yourself to do His will being done through you, even if it means suffering a premature physical death is a mystery to most of the body, so many have no idea as to who they truly are as a believer.

⁷ But <u>made himself of no reputation, and took upon him the form of a servant</u>, and <u>was made in the likeness of men</u>: ⁸ And being found in fashion as a man, he humbled himself, and became obedient unto death, even the death of the cross. ⁹ <u>Wherefore God also hath highly exalted him</u>, and <u>given him a name which is above every name</u>: ¹⁰ That at the name of Jesus every knee should bow, of things in heaven, and things in earth, and things under the earth; ¹¹ And that every tongue should confess that Jesus Christ is Lord, to the glory of God the Father.

Christ Dominion, not Domination

Now I know all of this sounds very strange, but one reason why is every denomination has its own formal doctrine that though it is typically scripture based to some degree it is also narrated to livingly support the tenants of faith they hold as its unique difference to all others.

Those who reveal God's will into this earth are revealing His very nature and essence. What is God's ***nature***? You could say it is His qualities and manner of disposition, the fundamental principles seen in how He governs revealed in His personality. What about His ***essence***? He is viewed as a *Living Spirit* revealed in His supernatural creative authority and power, which He has veiled in truths and righteousness as revealed in His glory.

Jesus appeared as a male of creation, having a *soul*, and yet was of the very *nature* and *essence* of the Father. The very *nature* of who Jesus was in heaven before His coming while still in the presence of the Father, was supernaturally conceived in Mary by the Spirit of God.

His true *essence* as a living *spirit* is just as His Father, yet He aligned himself with the Holy Spirit to occupy flesh. Therefore, He has the right to be called Gods first begotten Son, as it relates to before and after His physical birth as a man into this earth.

Math 28:18-20 *(GW) When Jesus came near, he spoke to them. He said, "All authority in heaven and on earth has been given to me. [19] So wherever you go, make disciples of all nations: Baptize them in the name of the Father, and of the Son, and of the Holy Spirit. [20] Teach them to do everything I have commanded you. "And remember that I am always with you until the end of time."*

Jesus reveals He has been given all authority in heaven and in earth and that we are to also by such an authority go forth and make disciples and baptize. He also tells us to teach them to do everything He had commanded us, and in His final statement He adds that He will be present with us always till the end of time.

However, His presence by the Holy Spirit is not to witness of himself to the unbeliever, but to witness to believers, His spiritual siblings who by their witness and testimony do the will of God. An important aspect to a believer fulfilling all this, it is that they must have the Holy Spirit working in and through them to fulfill it.

Now for any of you on the mediocrity fence pay close attention! No one can take Jesus out of the equation, He is the Son of God, He alone has done all to fulfill the Father's will in laying the foundation of salvation for all creation. In no way can I, or you, or anybody else, diminish His sufferings or the life He sacrificed by His love for us. What the Father required of Him He was willingly obedient and humbly submitted to fulfill therefore He is the only way, the only truth, and the only giver of life God in-visions for His offspring. He exalted Him for this and placed His name above all names to ever be named both in heaven and in earth.

He has also positioned Him as the spiritual head of the Church, through which He has purposed to reveal an authority and power in His name. His personal work of ministry on earth is finished, but He continues from a heavenly position as Chief Priest and Intercessor. He is before the Father daily revealing our personal work of ministry as offspring in the family of God. This 2000-year dispensation of the Church is still here, it is not over yet. Thus, your life in Christ is to be one that reflects in every way possible the very truths the Spirit of God is revealing. Amen.

Rom 8:33-34 *[33] Who shall lay any thing to the charge of God's elect? It is God that justifieth. [34] Who is he that condemneth? It is Christ that died, yea rather, that is risen again, <u>who is even at the right hand of God, who also maketh intercession for us</u>.*

I must express you should know that over the centuries there has been spiritual forces at work not aligned to the Spirit of God, preventing many believers from becoming mature in knowledge and understanding of who they are in Christ.

The reason such forces exist is by leaderships acceptance of ill-favored doctrinal control, so out of fear they raise congregants who are immaturely aware of the truth of who they are. Since many doctrines supporting them do not carry the same truths as already seen by many of you who are reading this.

This continuance among leadership to uphold a statute authority is to this day done to govern congregant's spiritual wellbeing. Thus, denominations and religious organizations have always famed that they exist because of a discord that occurred, or they saw a more enlightened movement by scripture.

No matter how they came about each has its own contrived doctrine to uphold and while most may be scripturally sound, they are not in total unity to God's doctrine.

Let us look at a scripture from the New Testament that has for centuries stymied many pastors, teachers, and other ministers of the gospel and yet nothing about it whether written in Greek or Hebrew or translated in this message format, reveals anything but the truth.

2 Cor 12:6-21 *(MSG)* *6 If I had a mind to brag a little, I could probably do it without looking ridiculous, and I'd still be speaking plain truth all the way. But I'll spare you. I don't want anyone imagining me as anything other than the fool you'd encounter if you saw me on the street or heard me talk. 7 Because of the extravagance of those revelations, and so I wouldn't get a big head, I was given the gift of a handicap to keep me in constant touch with my limitations. Satan's angel did his best to get me down; what he in fact did was push me to my knees. No danger then of walking around high and mighty!*

I am sure you figured out by now this is Paul writing about his thorn in the flesh that has as I said, for centuries been a focus of sort of eye disease, his physical stature, Jewish falsehoods, and/or a spirit of demonic influence, etc., etc.

The fact what did occur as revealed in these scriptures never is the true issue about them, it is always about theological pretext of a doctrinal sort to confound the knowledge of those they influence. Though the issue of variance among doctrines does not usually split churches it is one that virally confounds many believers as they hear all these interpretations from pulpits each enticed to deliver their own theological or doctrinal narrative or that of the denomination.

8 At first I didn't think of it as a gift, and begged God to remove it. Three times I did that, 9 and then he told me, My grace is enough; it's all you need. My strength comes into its own in your weakness. Once I heard that, I was glad to let it happen. I quit focusing on the handicap and began appreciating the gift. It was a case of Christ's strength moving in on my weakness.

What is important for every believer to know is, whatever is said by doctrinally empowered pulpits usually delivers messages that are not scripturally correct in context because it is aligned with supporting a doctrine that came from men.

[10] Now I take limitations in stride, and with good cheer, these limitations that cut me down to size—abuse, accidents, opposition, bad breaks. I just let Christ take over! And so the weaker I get, the stronger I become.

However, there is one who knows all truth and He is the Spirit of God whom Jesus calls the Spirit of truth.

John 16:13-15 *[13] Howbeit when he, the Spirit of truth, is come, he will guide you into all truth: for he shall not speak of himself; but whatsoever he shall hear, that shall he speak: and he will shew you things to come.*

He is not only going to reveal all truths regarding scripture, but also reveal things yet to come into the presence of those who are the Church. The thing believers need to focus upon is, no matter the ministry, no matter the denomination, no matter the seminary, and no matter the bible college, and finally no matter the church and its dynamics of ministry, if not led by the Spirit of God it is incorrect.

[14] He shall glorify me: for he shall receive of mine, and shall shew it unto you. [15] All things that the Father hath are mine: therefore said I, that he shall take of mine, and shall shew it unto you.

When I say incorrect, I am talking about foundational powers undergirding its efforts must be toward all its members or students or congregants totally bound to the truth of God's word. This is very important to the effectiveness of the gospel and the work of ministry so that a supernatural power confirms what is happening as seen by those in the world.

An unfortunate aspect is these different religious organizations and denominations that exists today reveal there are only a hand full that operate by the Spirit and the word. I know your questioning how I determined this, so how about we apply some more spiritual sense and see if you find it as I do.

Titus 2:1-15 *[1] But speak thou <u>the things which become sound doctrine</u>: [2] That the aged men be sober, grave, temperate, sound in faith, in charity, in patience. [3] The aged women likewise, that they be in behaviour as becometh holiness, not false accusers, not given to much wine, <u>teachers of good things</u>;*

Powers sanctioned around doctrines of men is a false power, as it is not sound in truths pertaining to the doctrine of God. When we look at scripture, we see a common thread running through every aspect of it, and that is all of it is based on a platform of truths God revealed by the Holy Spirit.

Thus, no matter whether it is in the Old Testament, or the New Testament all of it is written to reveal what God determined should be known.

[4] That they may teach the young women to be sober, to love their husbands, to love their children, [5] To be discreet, chaste, keepers at home, good, obedient to their own husbands, <u>that the word of God be not blasphemed</u>. [6] Young men likewise exhort to be sober minded. [7] In all things shewing thyself a <u>pattern of good works</u>: <u>in doctrine shewing uncorruptness, gravity, sincerity,</u>

Nothing He does is based on a lie or any deceiving mannerism, because if it were, God would not be who He is. As we see in the next verses there is to be no acceptance of condemnation of these truths and no manner of evil conversation is to be present in them.

[8] Sound speech, that cannot be condemned; that he that is of the contrary part may be ashamed, having no evil thing to say of you.

⁹ Exhort servants to be obedient unto their own masters, and to please them well in all things; not answering again; ¹⁰ Not purloining, but shewing all good fidelity; that <u>they may adorn the doctrine of God our Saviour in all things</u>.

Whatever God says is good for all in this now life of the flesh. So, I ask you; What do all believers really need? Is it these various denominations and the doctrines they uphold, or a Church unified and fully versed in a doctrine capable of all good things?

The answer is simple, as each of the others exists by humanist enforcements established to support its so-called spiritual existence. If this were not true, then no matter the name above the door the same doctrine based upon the same truths would be revealed by those transformed to be righteous sons and daughters of God.

You could say the proof is in the pudding, because you cannot grow up in an Assembly of God church learning about foundational perspectives applied therein and then go to a Methodist or Baptist or non-denominational and find the same doctrinal ideals in place.

So, while Christ may be at the center of many of them, they have built a spirit of ministry that encircles the sacrifice Jesus made but at the same time entangles the truth with not so true man-made interpretations gleaned to support egos committed to sustaining a doctrinal dominance.

¹¹ For the grace of God that bringeth salvation hath appeared <u>to all men</u>, ¹² <u>Teaching us that</u>, denying ungodliness and worldly lusts, we should live soberly, righteously, and godly, in this present world; ¹³ Looking for that blessed hope, and the glorious appearing of the great God and our Saviour Jesus Christ; ¹⁴ Who gave himself for us, that he might redeem us from all iniquity, and purify unto himself a peculiar people, zealous of good works. ¹⁵ <u>These things speak</u>, and <u>exhort</u>, and <u>rebuke with all authority</u>. <u>Let no man despise thee</u>.

There are many reasons why spiritual mediocrity is continuing to exist, seen in what should be known as revealed by the Holy Spirit from God's doctrine. Every believer has an inherited right to truth, and no one not even the devil himself has a right to deny them or anyone else receiving it. Clearly your spiritual wellbeing is all about Christ and an everlasting DOMINION, that at its foundation relies upon power flowing through you.

Dominion vs Domination

CHAPTER SIX

Spiritual Revival, Period

As I have already mentioned the spiritual wellbeing of God's family is dependent upon His offspring being reverent of their time here revealing His very nature and essence by living in a spiritually healthy manner. Along with this is to also be living mentally and emotionally healthy while in a fleshly body, reaping the promise of divine health.

Rom 8:9-19 *(NKJV) But you are not in the flesh but in the Spirit, if indeed the Spirit of God dwells in you. Now if anyone does not have the Spirit of Christ, he is not His.*

Here is evidence from the word of God that a habitation of the Holy Spirit is to be within God's children, and is to be their present state, so they will be revealed as those who are His.

10 And if Christ is in you, the body is dead because of sin, but the Spirit is life because of righteousness.

Christ in a believer because of His righteousness is to be their now manner of life, even though the physical body is still dying the Holy Spirit who raised Christ from the dead inhabits their own body.

Thus, a believer's physical body will be made alive with all vitality, strength, and agility, for as long as they choose to occupy it up to God's prophetic term of 120 years.

[11] But <u>if the Spirit of Him who raised Jesus from the dead dwells in you</u>, <u>He who raised Christ from the dead will also give life to your mortal bodies through His Spirit who dwells in you</u>. [12] Therefore, brethren, we are debtors--not to the flesh, to live according to the flesh. [13] For if you live according to the flesh you will die; but if by the Spirit you put to death the deeds of the body, you will live.

No longer are they to be indebted to live a life according to any dictates of the flesh. But are to live according to the Holy Spirit, putting to death all practical living by the flesh, and live as eternally alive *spirits* having a *soul* while occupying a fleshly *body*.

[14] For <u>as many as are led by the Spirit of God</u>, <u>these are sons of God</u>. [15] For you did not receive the spirit of bondage again to fear, but you received the Spirit of adoption by whom we cry out, "Abba, Father."

As members of the family of God they are to be led to live their lives according to the Holy Spirit who inhabits them. His habitation is not for the purpose of binding them as slaves to God's ways, but to bring them to freely live as God's own spiritual children.

[16] The <u>Spirit Himself bears witness with our spirit that we are children of God</u>, [17] and if children, then heirs--<u>heirs of God and joint heirs with Christ</u>, if indeed we suffer with Him, that we may also be glorified together.

There is no need for a believer to doubt any of this because the Holy Spirit will bear witness that they are truly a son or daughter of God. And since they are to reveal themselves as His child they will suffer as Christ suffered for living a life in this world according to their true family heritage.

Clearly, we see the word of truth has something to be revealed regarding who those in Christ truly are, thus, believers need to learn about how such a stature is obtained and kept fervent in the spiritual sense, so they are living free of mediocrity able to fulfill all works according to the Spirit in them.

Christ The First Truth, Then Us

Every believer has the same inheritance through faith in Christ. And as He was glorified or should I say exalted by His living His life in the flesh according to the Spirit of God so are we as children of God glorified, or exalted, by living our life according to the Spirit.

[18] For I consider that the sufferings of this present time are not worthy to be compared with the glory which shall be revealed in us,

As Christians we suffer persecution and ridicule by the world, simply because we are living a life that is so different to those who choose to live by the world's way, since it reveals the sin in their way of living. We suffer this for the Spirit of God to have liberty in us to do the will of the Father, since the result of such suffering is unable to compare to the glory revealed through us in this world.

[19] For the earnest expectation of the creation eagerly waits for the revealing of the sons of God.

The whole of the creation of God is eagerly waiting for such a manifestation on this earth. Our revealing is evident by willingness to live a life according to the Spirit not the world. As the purpose for the Holy Spirits being in the earth far exceeds our understanding, He alone enables an ability to manifest the glory of salvation through faith in Jesus Christ.

If we look at this as it is presented in the passion translation, we see there is a strong emphasis on this revealing to not only the world but also the whole universe.

Rom 8:19 *(TPT)* *The <u>entire universe is standing on tiptoe</u>, yearning <u>to see the unveiling of God's glorious sons and daughters</u>! ²⁰ For against its will the universe itself has had to endure the empty futility resulting from the consequences of human sin. But now, with eager expectation, ²¹ all creation longs for freedom from its slavery to decay and to experience with us the wonderful freedom coming to God's children.*

Jesus while here in the flesh had persecution and ridicule for His way of life. And yet He chose to live by or according to the Holy Spirit, while He lived with His disciples and walked with them and talked with them, presenting himself as the Son of Man, though He was the Son of God.

He was born a male of humanity having *spirit*, *soul*, and *body*, but living divinely without an indebtedness to His flesh, Thus, He was committed to living by a nature within Him aligned to the Father's. Christians who try and balance life by mediocre spirituality do so with an abundance of worldly thought and emotions added to any perception of truths.

God is not revealing how-to live-in Christ based on any world view, but on one that is founded on revelation truths.

Isa 55:8-9 *(NKJV)* *"For <u>My thoughts are not your thoughts</u>, Nor are your ways My ways," says the LORD. ⁹ "For as the heavens are higher than the earth, So are My ways higher than your ways, And My thoughts than your thoughts.*

Thank God, His ways and His thoughts are far above ours or we can say originate from a higher place. For His spiritual purposes are only revealed by revelation knowledge. So, our revealing the work of the Holy Spirit by knowledge of our true family heritage reveals we live by spiritual standards. Standards that today appear mediocre as activity in this season of pulpits blends the gospel with worldly ways.

Math 11:27-30 ^(AMP) *All things have been entrusted and delivered to Me by My Father; and <u>no one fully knows and accurately understands the Son except the Father</u>, and <u>no one fully knows and accurately understands the Father except the Son and anyone to whom the Son deliberately wills to make Him known</u>.*

Jesus says no one fully knows and understands Him, only the Father does, and clearly none of us fully know and understand the Father unless He willingly reveals Him to those who have a revived spirit capable of receiving revelation of it.

²⁸ Come to Me, all you who labor and are heavy-laden and overburdened, and I will cause you to rest. [I will ease and relieve and refresh your souls.] ²⁹ Take My yoke upon you and learn of Me, for I am gentle (meek) and humble (lowly) in heart, and you will find rest (relief and ease and refreshment and recreation and blessed quiet) for your souls.

Jesus makes it known that it requires a supernatural posture to participate in the purpose of His coming. He says to them take my yoke, *His way of living by the Spirit of God*, and learn of Me, and you will have peace of *souls*.

³⁰ For My yoke is wholesome (useful, good—not harsh, hard, sharp, or pressing, but comfortable, gracious, and pleasant), and My burden is light and easy to be borne.

His yoke or living by the Spirit not only provides rest, but a life as He says is wholesome, meaning it comes without any harshness, hardness, sharpness, or any pressing issues of the drama of life. For believers, being comfortable in God's fullness of grace is enough for us. But why speak these words to His disciples and those who were present? I believe it is because the leaders of that present generation at His coming, abided in religious ideals and hardness of heart as a way of life for those who believed in God.

Jesus assures all who are present in His name will come to know the true Father, and by receiving Him as the Son of God they would find rest and comfort for their *souls*.

One benefit to being led by the Holy Spirit is knowing and understanding who Christ's and your heavenly Father truly are, as this is essential to you having any spiritual wellbeing God decreed for you as His offspring. Believers must see themselves by faith as God sees them, sons and daughters who are led by the Holy Spirit.

1 John 2:20-27 *(AMP)* *But you have been anointed by [you hold a sacred appointment from, you have been given an unction from] the Holy One, and you all know [the Truth] or you know all things.*

The anointing John is revealing here is because believers have a sacred appointment of the Holy Spirit abiding in and with each of them, and He is the only one revealing truths from the word of God. These truths are revealed because they are anointed to be perceptive of what they need to know and how none of it is false.

21 I write to you not because you are ignorant and do not perceive and know the Truth, but because you do perceive and know it, and [know positively] that nothing false (no deception, no lie) is of the Truth.

No believer is to be ignorant of any truth God has determined to be revealed to them, since the Holy Spirit is raising them up to have perception of it, so that they know what is untrue regarding the world and what it says about God.

22 Who is [such a] liar as he who denies that Jesus is the Christ (the Messiah)? He is the antichrist (the antagonist of Christ), who [habitually] denies and refuses to acknowledge the Father and the Son. 23 No one who [habitually] denies (disowns) the Son even has the Father. Whoever confesses (acknowledges and has) the Son has the Father also.

Only those who have a spirit of antichrist deny that Jesus is the Messiah, the Son of God, but those who confess and acknowledge Jesus as the Son of God have the Father as their own. Their own what? SPIRITUAL FATHER. This is a very significant statement since everyone is either of the devil or of God.

Every son and daughter of God must hang on to truth that was revealed in the beginning of their faith in Christ. Because if they do, they have a place in the hierarchal presence of the Father in His Son.

24 As for you, keep in your hearts what you have heard from the beginning. If what you heard from the first dwells and remains in you, then you will dwell in the Son and in the Father [always].

God in revealing His word shows us He has promised that we who have chosen to accept the truth of it are revealed by the Spirit of God as those having eternal life.

25 And this is what He Himself has promised us—the life, the eternal [life]. 26 I write this to you with reference to those who would deceive you [seduce and lead you astray].

However, those who would be deceivers of truth do so for the purpose of edification of things not aligned to the doctrine of God causing believers to stray from truth. Many in the family have no perception of the things that will come in the last days of the Church, thus living presently void of any truths revealing it. Situations such as these occur because believers are made to accept the status queue.

27 But as for you, the anointing (the sacred appointment, the unction) which you received from Him abides [permanently] in you; [so] then you have no need that anyone should instruct you. But just as His anointing teaches you concerning everything and is true and is no falsehood, so you must abide in (live in, never depart from) Him [being rooted in Him, knit to Him], just as [His anointing] has taught you [to do].

That verse reveals there is an anointing present by the Holy Spirit's *occupation*, and by such an anointing one has no need for someone else to reveal truth. This does not mean they do not need to listen to or receive teaching from those He gifts to minister to them, but in doing so this anointing will ensure that they will know any truth revealed to them.

The Holy Spirit anoints believers to know all truth in anything He reveals, meaning it is not only about abiding in them, but them abiding in and being rooted in His anointed presence ensuring they know what they need to know when they need to know it.

Hosea 4:6 *My people are destroyed for lack of knowledge: because thou hast rejected knowledge, I will also reject thee, that thou shalt be no priest to me: seeing thou hast forgotten the law of thy God, I also will forget thy children.*

Many of you have read these scriptures about Israel and how a lack of knowledge led them to tribulation and destruction. There are several things revealed here but first look at the main subject matter which is, *knowledge*.

In the below scripture we see whatever wisdom is revealed from God, it is right and nothing in it is contrary to any truth. And since everything is revealed through knowledge and understanding it is to be a paramount aspect of a believer's life as a righteous child of God. Now keep focus as I go through this; It is revealed knowledge and has a value that is above understanding. Why?

Prov 8:8-10 *(AMP)All the words of my mouth are righteous (upright and in right standing with God); there is nothing contrary to truth or crooked in them. ⁹They are all plain to him who understands [and opens his heart], and right to those who find knowledge [and live by it]. ¹⁰Receive my instruction in preference to [striving for] silver, and knowledge rather than choice gold,*

Because *knowledge* brings forth the facts by truths that justify such knowing to the extent, we have faith in it. U*nderstanding* is for having perceived its purpose, limits, and applications in one's heart. And *wisdom* is for an ability to apply knowledge and understanding for good works God proposed.

Eph 2:10 *[10] For we are his workmanship, created in Christ Jesus unto good works, which God hath before ordained that we should walk in them.*

Knowledge in scripture is often seen as more important than understanding as it expounds on us and what we say as result of our learning it, this is precious to God. We as His family, must learn from our past and the mistakes many have made in our being in lack of knowledge to these truths. Because it reveals how we have ended up in mediocrity among an unbelieving mass of evil doers.

Prov 20:15 *(AMP) There is gold, and a multitude of pearls, but the lips of knowledge are a vase of preciousness [the most precious of all].*

The world's opinion of the family of God as the Church appears to be made up of what they hear and see because the Church looks no different than the world from many of those who clearly are a part of it.

Eze 36:19 *And I scattered them among the heathen, and they were dispersed through the countries: according to their way and according to their doings I judged them.*

Mediocrity does not appear as an anointed posture and sets us apart from His purpose. The leaders of Israel were held accountable for lacking in truthful nurturing of His nation, but He also held all Israel accountable for sin because of lacking in knowledge of Him.

Amos 3:1-2 *(MSG) Listen to this, Israel. GOD is calling you to account—and I mean all of you, everyone connected with the family*

117

that he delivered out of Egypt. Listen! [2]"Out of all the families on earth, I picked you. Therefore, because of your special calling, <u>I'm holding you responsible for all your sins</u>."

In the age of the Church, we are no longer under a dispensation of judgment, but under grace He has chosen to express toward us by revelation knowledge. But an accountability of such knowledge has not been removed, the Lord has declared none of us are to judge each other, as all of us will give an account of our life to Him at the end.

Knowledge from God's word is knowledge not born of any earthly nature, but knowledge to reveal His Divine nature, as His power is inherently crafted into His word to transform our nature by the Spirit of God. As I stated, there must be transformation of *soul* taking place in every son and daughter of God on a spiritual level by knowledge of truth as revealed by the Holy Spirit from the word.

The problem many believers have today is church pulpits and ministries have removed any working of the Holy Spirit. Why? It is because more and more of those who minister and those who are ministered to today are not inclined to lean to changes brought by the truths in the word of God.

There is a danger in doing this as it leaves believers void of the spiritual nutrients needed to be healthy and vibrant in the spirit. You cannot take the one who inspired those to write what is in scripture out of it, He is the revealer of truth, if you remove Him from His purpose of revealing it then you remove the testator and scripture becomes void of its promised power.

Many things written herein are not going to be accepted, that is obvious by whatever is going forth from pulpits as it is not effective in maturing the whole of His parts. Evident in the fact many today live without the knowledge and understanding they should have.

Though the world currently does not see such a revealing of the children of God, it can and must occur, since it reveals the truth that is contained in scripture.

Divine Nature is from God.

The message from pulpits of churches must be for the same purpose as God endeavors, to reveal by the Holy Spirit truths that transforms a creation of males and females into who He calls His spiritual offspring.

However, in talking about this there is something I need to hit head on, and that is believers were never to be as expendable assets of a church ministry or organization to be used and/or abused as leadership sees fit. Jesus as head of the Church has not changed anything, the purpose of it is the same as before its existence. But uncharacteristic mannerisms of late gives clear evidence some have strayed from this, and/or have no perception of it.

I can clarify this, bringing the issue of dark arenas and dynamic praise into view. Here we have churches and organizations that have deemed the God of light abides in the darkness, and abuse the talents of those who they parade around in front of 50ft LED screens while singing songs that are past the edge of true praise and worship.

Anyone who sees believers as a disposable asset of the ministry is not equipped with any love God exercises and fit for pulpit or otherwise. Since believers are to partake as the word says, in the knowledge of Christ and the Father according to His Divine power that gives all things pertaining to life and godliness.

All of this comes through the knowledge of God and is a result of offspring who are not just recipients of His great and glorious promises, or mere spectators of the results of His blessings of others. But those who actively partake of a Divine nature that brings an escape from the world's corruption within.

2 Peter 1:1-4 Simon Peter, a servant and an apostle of Jesus Christ, to them that have obtained like precious faith with us through the righteousness of God and our Saviour Jesus Christ: [2] Grace and peace be multiplied unto you through the knowledge of God, and of Jesus our Lord, [3] According as his divine power hath given unto us all things that pertain unto life and godliness, through the knowledge of him that hath called us to glory and virtue: [4] Whereby are given unto us exceeding great and precious promises: that by these ye might be partakers of the divine nature, having escaped the corruption that is in the world through lust.

A change is coming to the family, and it is a change that will reveal the true nature and character of the God who gave the right for us to be His offspring. And with it a change in the corporate wellbeing of the Church reflected in our personal change brought about by the Holy Spirit.

This book and everything in it are not written for the purpose of me laying out the specific details on any life areas, but more on our responsibility as His offspring to allow the Holy Spirit to be an intricate part of our daily living. He is revealing what God has written in His word for our knowledge and understanding regarding who we are and how we are to be through His eyes, so that we are without any spiritual mediocrity.

Therefore, the Church must occupy, or more correctly to keep ourselves busy till He comes, in so doing we will be without this mediocre spirit fulfilling His expectation of us as His offspring. This also requires our having all areas of our living essence here be in peace and harmony to every aspect of truth, even those that reveal our personal families are a part of the process to bring about a mature stature as Christ. So, every effort must be made within God's family and yours to ensure this will occur, since an environment where God's word is within it an ability to transform the nature of everyone is present.

Now you do not have to agree with me on what I say in the next few paragraphs, but I think you will know perfectly well what I am talking about. The today Church struggles to manifest its purpose, and is no longer seen by this world as having spiritual propriety, instead it is seen as hypocritical and falsely testifying of itself.

It is also seen as cowering under a mainstream mannerism of spiritual prowess, secure in its position in Christ, yet struggling to live in any victorious manner in aspects of it. So, before you blow your holy gaskets over this let us try and be spiritually sensible in learning of it.

The fact such a Church does exist is by many reasons, first there is a fundamental lack of truths coming from pulpits, and second as congregants are unaware of accountability, third they are very weak in spiritual wellbeing. This makes the process of a transformed nature difficult, but not impossible, thus, the Holy Spirit is writing about this spiritual mediocrity, because if it continues an image of God will not.

I said it is not so much about the details of these things as it is the processes available in the word to bring one's nature to apply His principles. He has no intention of believers struggling to be victorious, but it requires them having perception of how He deals with them pertaining to spiritual wellbeing as part of God's family.

It is all part of a process for occupying by the Spirit a place in His Church, where spiritual maturity is key to an eternal plan. Many churches declare all their congregation is just one big family, yet in that family are many struggling to be a Christian and survive this present age of hate, and cancel culture.

Concern for a wellbeing of congregants is today being attended to by magisterially scheduled programs edifying the pulpit as sole source of spirit nurturing. Thus, the congregation sits as life wearied souls only good for tithes and offerings.

It is time for every believer to take responsibility for who they are and bring back a true unity of reviving the body of Christ, as in the days of the early Church. Where everyone's wellbeing was a daily consideration essential to its spiritual whole-being.

John 3:14-16 *(ISV)* *Just as Moses lifted up the serpent in the wilderness,* <u>*so must the Son of Man be lifted up,*</u> *15*<u>*so that everyone who believes in him would have eternal life.*</u> *16"For this is how God loved the world: He gave his uniquely existing Son so that everyone who believes in him would not be lost but have eternal life.*

Our occupation as the Church on this earth is temporary, but it is an occupation required for a preparation of an eternal one that brings a new one. God determined a 2000-year age of time be set apart for revealing those who are inherently occupied by the Spirit of God, as spiritual images of Him.

Gen 1:2 *And the earth was without form, and void; and darkness was upon the face of the deep. And the* <u>*Spirit of God*</u> *moved upon the face of the waters.*

Nothing is done on earth or to the earth as a part of God's plan unless the Spirit of God does it, whether by himself or through those He chooses. As He orchestrates the will of the Father the power of God to fulfill what has already been spoken occurs, thus bringing to pass the very eternal plans laid out from the beginning.

Gen 41:38 *And Pharaoh said unto his servants, Can we find such a one as this is, a man in whom the* <u>*Spirit of God*</u> *is?*

He works through those who are obedient to the Father's will to do as He instructs for the benefit of them and those He wants to bless in the process.

2 Chron15:1 *And the* <u>*Spirit of God*</u> *came upon Azariah the son of Oded:*

Even amid God's wrath He will call on those who are willing to be used by the Spirit of God for a deliverance from it to reveal His glory on earth.

2 Chron 24:20 And the Spirit of God came upon Zechariah the son of Jehoiada the priest, which stood above the people, and said unto them, Thus saith God, Why transgress ye the commandments of the LORD, that ye cannot prosper? because ye have forsaken the LORD, he hath also forsaken you.

By the Spirit of God, the prophets of old spoke as the Father to the nation of Israel to bring a surrender to His commandments and the blessings He had afforded them from the beginning.

Math 12:28 But if I cast out devils by the Spirit of God, then the kingdom of God is come unto you.

Jesus removed the evil forces at work in the people of God in His day and did so by the anointing that abided through the presence of the Holy Spirit. The same thing still happens today through those who are willing to be a vessel anointed to do the will of God.

Rom 15:19 Through mighty signs and wonders, by the power of the Spirit of God; so that from Jerusalem, and round about unto Illyricum, I have fully preached the gospel of Christ.

God reveals himself through those whom the Spirit empowers, He today is empowering His offspring by an occupation of the same Spirit to reveal a Divine nature. No prophecy in scripture defines the current level of spiritual mediocrity the Church is filled with thus showing us we need to get a revival of truth for what has been and is yet to be revealed.

Revival occurs when the work of the Holy Spirit is present, and no denomination or any religious organization of late or group of people or even the most dynamic of ministries can muster up the power and authority required to revive the body of Christ.

Spiritual Revival, Period

CHAPTER SEVEN

Prominence of Faith

Let me make this comment up front; Churches who actively help congregants in spiritual areas by providing classes or teachings on faith and the dangers of doubt that affects them becoming a more effective child of God are all doing the will of God. However, in reviewing this issue of faith I found that in many churches today it is a conflictive topic. As the spiritual aspects of faith today reveals a promotion of ignorance to certain truths about God's way of life leaving congregants living by a level of maturity that is mediocre at best.

So, since I made that statement, I should vilify it if possible. I was recently watching videos of church services where many of the pastors were of the younger generational trend who promote the dynamics of services we see today. What I noticed was majority of them presented messages that were exceptional in the aspects of biblical exhortation as they used scripture to tie together the message they were ministering. But the messages were all about drama living or what I should say is issues created by emotional reactions to life situations such as finances, relationships, or more often social fails people go through in life. While ministering on these type issues is relevant the thing that was missing was practical teaching on faith.

Now to start with we need to acknowledge there are those on one end of the spectrum of faith holding onto and expressing an acceptance of the extensively revealed faith messages that came along in the late 60's on into the 80's. And on the other end is those who are in poverty of truths and minded of only seeing faith to name it and claim it, revealing a marginal dexterity of doctrine has been issued. And then there are those we can assume are somewhere in between prayerfully.

What makes faith important to a believer is, it is the one element God factors into everything He does, so there is an importance of it being in His creation of men and women to ensure they align to His will. Faith is also the governing factor for scriptural truths the Holy Spirit reveals concerning one receiving it, growing it, and how to use it.

Rom 10:17 *17 So then faith cometh by hearing, and hearing by the word of God.*

So, it is important believers perceive God is the source of all things they will ever need, and that there are principles associated to processes of obtaining it by faith in His word. Faith is not something believers make happen on their own it is a result of the spiritual blessings of God purposed for every believer living a righteous life by the presence of the Holy Spirit. And since faith comes from God it is connected to a supernatural realm of power, that makes the word a principle means for revelation truths to increase its working.

Rom 12:3 *3 For I say, through the grace given unto me, to every man that is among you, not to think of himself more highly than he ought to think; but to think soberly, according as God hath dealt to every man the measure of faith.*

For anyone to receive and correctly fulfill their part in His plan living in this New Covenant there must be a faithful dependence upon God being the resource for all things both spiritual and natural.

Everywhere in scripture especially where spiritual blessings are concerned there is emphasis on His multiplying them for a purpose of bestowing benefits upon others, He sees in need of what they will provide. This is an important principle the body of Christ needs to have perception of so that its purpose will be fulfilled in the way God perceived in the beginning.

However, when it comes to faith many define it to operate to the degree enabling what they seek after which often is a prosperity of finances and health for themselves. Such blessings are available by faith but why are so many of His children not abundantly wealthy and/or healthy and highly effective in spiritual matters? I believe, it is because for every area of God's blessing there is to be a spiritually perceived purpose that one must know concerning not only how to receive blessings but how to be willing to distribute them.

Prosperity is a principle that requires faith in God, the same kind of faith He applies to himself, and has revealed to us in everything He does, when faith works this principle will bring a prosperity of *soul*.

3 John 1:2 *(AMP) Beloved, I pray that <u>you may prosper in all things and be in health</u>, just as your soul prospers.*

It is God's will we prosper in all things, but prospering and being in health is associated to a *soul* being prosperous, it is not only about blessings of wealth, riches, and health. It is having all needs and/or circumstances met with whatever is required to fulfill them. Faith is a key principle used in this process and it is paramount to everyone receiving anything from God.

But concerning money many are caught up in the ability of it, and not in the ability of God to provide for them. As a result, they end up living life constantly seeking financial increase but still are remaining void of its blessings.

Thus, regarding prosperity, if the results are a craving for riches some even to the point of *lusting* after it, then faith is not a part of the process. If we look at Paul in the New Testament, we can see something different. His understanding about being prospered was for spiritual purposes, in that his prayer request were not so he could do what he wanted, but do what God wanted.

Rom 1:9-11 For God is my witness, whom I serve with my spirit in the gospel of his Son, that without ceasing I make mention of you always in my prayers; ¹⁰ Making request, if by any means now at length I might have a prosperous journey by the will of God to come unto you. ¹¹ For I long to see you, that I may impart unto you some spiritual gift, to the end ye may be established;

His thinking of prosperity coming from God was to provide blessings that he could use to help deliver a spiritual encouragement and strength, thus revealing and establishing righteousness in those he witnessed to. He understood the principle of faith, in that beyond his personal needs which God would meet, was a spiritual purpose that his Father was focused upon, and Paul was faithfully confident God's blessings were sufficient to do it.

Another key thing is, a blessing of the Lord that makes one rich, means anything we do by any laborious effort of our own will add nothing to it.

Prov 10:22 (AMP) 22 The blessing of the Lord—it makes [truly] rich, and He adds no sorrow with it [neither does toiling increase it].

Every believer's faith is secured in the supernatural realm of God and placed in each one making them fully capable of obtaining spiritual results He is after. Faith is not a natural part of us when birthed into this earthly realm, though faith may be used in some natural means, by the word of God it brings forth forces that are like no other on earth.

Whatever is manifested is by the Spirit supernaturally produced and determined to be for spiritual purposes God has ordained to occur by the one applying it. Yet it is possible that spiritual purpose God determined are cut off if the principles of faith are not applied.

Today's churches place uncharacteristic burdens on the faith of those who attend seen in the effort leadership puts forth for a continuance of tithes and offerings. It is the method of request that conflicts with God's principles for giving since they are often made not for spirit led works, but for an economic process that hinders the purpose of faith.

Most congregations have no idea of the financial burdens they are being asked to faithfully fulfill. But they typically respond to the offering time expecting what they give will be used in a right manner regarding the church's ministry and liabilities. This process is out of character to many of the principles God operates by, as each member complies to a so-called spirit led effort that is worldly. I know you are saying so what if the Church uses an economic system to operate, how else can it be done? I assure you there are principles God has that if applied to <u>His</u> *tithes*, and *offerings* would bring an opened window of heaven type abundance of blessing.

Mal 3:10 *(AMP)* *10 Bring all the tithes (the whole tenth of your income) into the storehouse, that there may be food in My house, and prove Me now by it, says the Lord of hosts, <u>if I will not open the windows of heaven for you and pour you out a bless</u>ing, that <u>there shall not be room enough to receive it</u>.*

Christ never intended for His Church to be built on economics indebted to a worldly Babylonian system. His economics operate on kingdom principles having spiritual perspectives at work by faith. Church leadership must see it is Jesus who gave His life to lay down a spiritual foundation of which He is the chief cornerstone, and by faith every effort must apply principles God endeavors to operate.

Though there will be requirements of money, material goods, and individual laborers in fulfilling His purpose, it is to be for the use of the Holy Spirit to bring about what the Father has already perceived to be done.

Every disciple Jesus sent out, which included the twelve, were empowered and anointed with authority to operate in the very same way He operated. This required faith in the truth He had told and showed them would occur by the power of God. They healed the sick, cast out demons all being demonstrations of power along with preaching and teaching the gospel or good news. And everything was done using principles shown to them and us from scripture revealing God's intent and concern is revealing His plan of salvation through Jesus His Son.

Math 10:8-11 *(MSG)* *Bring* <u>*health to the sick*</u>. <u>*Raise the dead*</u>. <u>*Touch the untouchables*</u>. <u>*Kick out the demons*</u>. *You have been treated generously, so live generously.* ⁹ *"Don't think you have to put on a fund-raising campaign before you start.* ¹⁰ *You don't need a lot of equipment. You are the equipment, and all you need to keep that going is three meals a day. Travel light.* ¹¹ *"When you enter a town or village, don't insist on staying in a luxury inn. Get a modest place with some modest people, and be content there until you leave.*

Faith endowed with spiritual blessings enables it to accomplish what God intends to happen. This is all believers need, they do not need a week or weeks to plan out every detail and take offerings to raise all the funds or take a whole store of things. But go and by faith allow the Spirit of God to use them, not having any desire to stay in expensive places, but be content in whatever is offered. Jesus will never send us out to do something that is different from what His Father prophesied would occur. Believers are to flow in His same working of the Holy Spirit, so that there is no deviation from any spiritual purpose that the Father has perceived will come to pass.

These are principles revealed by Jesus the builder of His Church that pertain to believers going forth ministering the gospel for the harvest of *souls*. And they make it clear that in going forth to do the same works requires <u>faith</u> to trust God to provide whatever is needed to fulfill such an effort.

However, there in lies a problem this is not happening at the level of spiritual activity it should be most especially in the churches of this country. This a result of lack of faith or unknown truths that require faith to bring about God's will. That does not mean there is no ministry occurring as the gospel is continuing to be heard but the gospel of today is filtered through worldly principles making faith a byproduct and not the main ingredient.

Faith is not to do what we want but to do what God wants therefore, we could say the purpose of faith is for manifesting the intent and concern in the heart of the Father over His creation. And the anointing and power that is of God requires one only have the faith He provides that grows by the word and the Holy Spirit.

A very important aspect in the annals of faith, is for you to know how an individual or churches are to be led by the Spirit of God to fulfill ministerial tasks. Based on this fact; Jesus never veers away from a spiritual purpose His Father has determined to be done. Many believe Jesus's ministry was poor, mainly in the aspects of finances and faith among His disciples, when in fact it was very prosperous not only by economic standards but by the faith standards that reveal they operated in the power of God.

This is vastly different to how ministries operate today in using monetary gifts they so diligently seek after to support the work of it. As I mentioned, churches and ministries historically place more and more demands on the faith of God's children without any teaching, preaching, and exhorting truth to increase it by the work of the Holy Spirit and the word.

I know what many say concerning doing the work of ministry is for the Church it must be able to plan out how such works will occur prayerfully led by the Spirit of God! Yes, the Lord is working at the spiritual root in the works to be done, and He is prophetically bound to provide all things required to align it to God's plan.

Way too many church leaders of today act like members only grow their faith by believing for more money to do whatever work they determined for them to associate faith to. And no effort is being put forth at pulpits to support increasing the faith of the congregants to know how God fulfills it.

This shows leaders have more faith in the members ability to get it done than in God's ability, thus they themselves lack in the faith necessary to bring into manifestation the very will of the Father.

Faith by Hearing the Word

As the overall goal of ministry is to bring others to Christ, which is and always will be by a supernatural process of the Holy Spirit. It will at times require some natural means to accomplish, including money but this overwhelming concern by leadership for getting the money is what creates a real problem. Since the spiritual purpose to be considered is regarding those who are to be ministered to, and the congregants to be used by the Spirit of God to get it done.

Math 9:37-38 *[37] Then saith he unto his disciples, <u>The harvest truly is plenteous, but the labourers are few</u>; [38] Pray ye therefore the Lord of the harvest, that he will send forth labourers into his harvest.*

Jesus, said ask for more workers because the harvest is plenty but said nothing about money to those whom He chose in providing their own means to do so, money was not required. His focus was on what the Holy Spirit accomplishes by one person's faith not on what it will take to get there.

Math 10:1 [1] *And when he had called unto him his twelve disciples, he gave them power against unclean spirits, to cast them out, and to heal all manner of sickness and all manner of disease.*

The very thing believers are supposed to do is minister for a transformation of *soul* as faithful workers having the same intent and concern in their hearts as the Father. But the principles associated to doing this are not resting upon money or any works they provide, as everything is founded upon what God will do through each of them as His offspring by the Holy Spirit. The fact Jesus has sole oversight of it all, reveals He sees beyond the realm of time, and knows the needs of individuals and nations in advance.

Gen 22:15-18 [(AMP)] *In blessing I will bless you and in multiplying I will multiply your descendants like the stars of the heavens and like the sand on the seashore. And your Seed (Heir) will possess the gate of His enemies,*

There are two things revealed here for us to garner knowledge and understanding of regarding blessings from God. First: In this day of the Church those called sons and daughters of the Highest, by faith have a right to every manner of blessing He bestowed upon Abraham.

[18] *And in your Seed [Christ] shall all the nations of the earth be blessed and [by Him] bless themselves, because you have heard and obeyed My voice.*

This includes any natural resource for maintaining wellbeing of spirit, soul, and flesh or our natural health. And second: Blessings Abraham received were purposed for spiritual outcomes God had predetermined to occur, thus empowered to bless the one receiving. Abraham's blessings led to an increase in possessions that were multiplied exponentially because they were supernaturally sourced from a realm that is unseen.

The fact many ministries are in financial trouble today reveals there is a lack of truth for knowledge and understanding from God's word that grows faith regarding the type of wealth and riches He provides.

Rom 4:7-8 *[7]Blessed are those whose lawless deeds are forgiven, And whose sins are covered; [8] Blessed is the man to whom the LORD shall not impute sin*

The word translated blessed in the previous verse is the Greek word (***makarios***) from a root (***makarizō***) meaning "large, lengthy, and in this verse expressed, "to pronounce blessed," in other words all believers have been declared a position of increase or blessing. This cannot be deferred except by a lack of faith to receive them.

You should be shouting right now because you are positioned for increase and blessing you cannot receive by religious works or fulfill by doctrinal rituals, or reach elevated levels of theological prowess before what is yours by faith in Jesus is in your possession.

Mark 11:22-24 *[22] And Jesus answering saith unto them, Have faith in God. [23] For verily I say unto you, That whosoever shall say unto this mountain, Be thou removed, and be thou cast into the sea; and shall not doubt in his heart, but shall believe that those things which he saith shall come to pass; he shall have whatsoever he saith. [24] Therefore I say unto you, What things soever ye desire, when ye pray, believe that ye receive them, and ye shall have them.*

I am going to repeat this for your sake of understanding, since one's faith is not founded on what you say but on what God has said, it makes it "supernaturally" empowered. The above verse in another translation says have the faith of God, so whatever the translation the importance is faith is given to enable our ability to do something that in the natural we cannot do. In the case of blessings, it is to bring into presence a manifestation of something that exists in the realm of the Spirit only obtainable by faith.

Luke 12:28-31 [28] *If then God so clothe the grass, which is today in the field, and tomorrow is cast into the oven; how much more will he clothe you, O ye of little faith?* [29] *And seek not ye what ye shall eat, or what ye shall drink, neither be ye of doubtful mind.* [30] *For all these things do the nations of the world seek after: and your Father knoweth that ye have need of these things.* [31] *But rather seek ye the kingdom of God; and all these things shall be added unto you.*

Today many are seeking elevated levels of faith for things they are already blessed with but do not know. The reason He says to the disciples, oh ye of little faith, is because they struggle to keep faith over things in their life, they have very little of and it focuses them on the having and not on how faith will obtain it. It comes down to seeking the first things first, then receiving whatever else is needed.

There is an expectation by God for believers to be obedient in faith to the revealing of Christ the Son of God which before was hidden but now is made known through faith in the word of the prophets and commandments of God. This is so the power that is to be seen is freely flowing through those who by wisdom operate it.

Rom 16:25-26 [25] *Now to him that is of power to stablish you according to my gospel, and the preaching of Jesus Christ, according to the revelation of the mystery, which was kept secret since the world began,* [26] *But now is made manifest, and by the scriptures of the prophets, according to the commandment of the everlasting God, made known to all nations for the obedience of faith:*

This is not about us having some level of faith founded on our power or ability it is about faith that reveals the power and ability of God in the work of ministry regardless of what denomination or organization you associate with. I am tired of watching leaders treat their congregants as if they are the most spiritually ignorant persons who must be told what to do at every event in the process.

The reason any member of the church would not be perceiving of what they as a child of God are to do is because the leadership has not told them the truth. And in many instances do not intend to as it would bring those not called into their level of spiritual acuity.

1 Cor 2:2-11 2 For I determined not to know anything among you, save Jesus Christ, and him crucified. [3] And I was with you in weakness, and in fear, and in much trembling. [4] And my speech and my preaching was not with enticing words of man's wisdom, but in demonstration of the Spirit and of power: [5] That your faith should not stand in the wisdom of men, but in the power of God.

As Paul asserts above any who come to Christ because of one's ministry, witness, or testimony should occur by the manifestation of the power of God which is by faith of the one ministering. This is so those ministered to will have faith to receive the wisdom of it, and not have faith in the ministry who revealed it.

[6] Howbeit we speak wisdom among them that are perfect: yet not the wisdom of this world, nor of the princes of this world, that come to nought:

When a believer has increased their faith to the point, they are able to bring the power of God into manifestation it is not something that is going to be by any naturally known process. But by a process that requires perceiving the wisdom of it is for God's will to be done according to the promise.

[7] But we speak the wisdom of God in a mystery, even the hidden wisdom, which God ordained before the world unto our glory: [8] Which none of the princes of this world knew: for had they known it, they would not have crucified the Lord of glory.

As stated by the previous scripture this is wisdom not known by any worldly order of powers but wisdom that in the past hidden but if known Christ would not have been crucified.

Though this is in reference to Christ as the Son of God, it shows us if what can be known is hidden then actions will not be as God's will for His creation. Leadership not revealing truths necessary for faith grow may not be better than those mentioned above.

⁹ But as it is written, Eye hath not seen, nor ear heard, neither have entered into the heart of man, the things which God hath prepared for them that love him. ¹⁰ But <u>God hath revealed them unto us by his Spirit</u>: <u>for the Spirit searcheth all things, yea, the deep things of God</u>. ¹¹ For what man knoweth the things of a man, save the spirit of man which is in him? even so the things of God knoweth no man, but the Spirit of God.

Believers must be capable of perceiving the purpose of those things the Holy Spirit is making known to the Church in this day and hour. This requires an increased faith so what is revealed confirms it is aligned to God's will and since it is made known they clearly see that only He would know such things.

There is nothing that is so spiritually deep that He would keep it from us, when we by faith trust Him to be the revealer of it. And just as we have seen, nothing about faith accommodates mediocrity, but it is being purposed by pulpits who themselves are without faith in the ability of the Lord who presides over them.

Faith, All We Ever Need

__Heb 11:1-13__ ¹ Now <u>faith is the substance of things hoped for, the evidence of things not seen</u>. ² For <u>by it the elders obtained a good report</u>. ³ Through faith we understand that the worlds were framed by the word of God, so that things which are seen were not made of things which do appear.

Faith is a doorway to things unseen, and a gateway to knowing how God created all things out of nothing by using only the power of His word.

⁴ By faith Abel offered unto God a more excellent sacrifice than Cain, by which he obtained witness that he was righteous, God testifying of his gifts: and by it he being dead yet speaketh.

It is amazing that after the fall of Adam God still honored faith in that Abel's offering was counted as a witness of faith in the God who created Him. Where-in Cain's situation his faith was in his own ability to create the thing offered, not in the one he offered it to.

⁵ By faith Enoch was translated that he should not see death; and was not found, because God had translated him: for before his translation he had this testimony, that he pleased God. ⁶ But without faith it is impossible to please him: for he that cometh to God must believe that he is, and that he is a rewarder of them that diligently seek him.

Faith places us in a position where supernatural things will take place that are anointed for a witness throughout eternity. Enoch, had faith enough to believe he pleased God and because of it, God took him off the earth, transferring him to another place.

Faith must be of a nature it enables a believer to please God, but it also says they are to not only believe that He is who He is, but that He will reward them for diligently seeking after Him.

⁷ By faith Noah, being warned of God of things not seen as yet, moved with fear, prepared an ark to the saving of his house; by the which he condemned the world, and became heir of the righteousness which is by faith.

Noah and the flood, an interesting fact is he was moved out of fear of losing his family to do what God told him to do (build an Ark). But his faith in God doing what He said about a flood saved him and his family.

⁸ By faith Abraham, when he was called to go out into a place which he should after received for an inheritance, obeyed; and he went out, not knowing whither he went. ⁹By faith he sojourned in the land of promise, as in a strange country, dwelling in tabernacles with Isaac and Jacob, the heirs with him of the same promise: ¹⁰For he looked for a city which hath foundations, whose builder and maker is God.

Abraham continued to do whatever God told him to do even in a desert place where he was a foreigner. But he by faith continued to believe he and his descendants would inherit the promises of God even though the land he was standing in was strange to him.

¹¹ Through faith also Sara herself received strength to conceive seed, and was delivered of a child when she was past age, because she judged him faithful who had promised. ¹² Therefore sprang there even of one, and him as good as dead, so many as the stars of the sky in multitude, and as the sand which is by the seashore innumerable.

Sarah the wife of Abraham through faith received the refreshing of her flesh to the degree she was able to conceive when she was 90 years old and not only conceive but strength to carry the fetus whole term to the birth of Isaac. All because she by faith believed God to be faithful to fulfill the promise He made.

¹³ These all died in faith, not having received the promises, but having seen them afar off, and were persuaded of them, and embraced them, and confessed that they were strangers and pilgrims on the earth.

Everyone mentioned in scripture believed in what God said He would do by faith. It is never going to be about what we do here, outside of salvation through Christ, it is and always will be about what God does through those who have faith to trust Him to do exactly what He says. But if spiritual mediocrity is the status of a believer faith is not working to the degree needed for a life of blessing and health both in the natural and the supernatural.

The only way believers change from mediocrity to maturity is to get into alignment with truths contained in the word as they are revealed by the Holy Spirit. Since faith comes and increases only by a process of hearing words God crafts into them an ability to change.

Eph 4:13-24 [13] *Till we all come in the unity of the faith, and of the knowledge of the Son of God, unto a perfect man, unto the measure of the stature of the fulness of Christ:*

Everything God is doing is to keep His offspring alive and well *spirit, soul,* and *body* for a purpose of blessing them and those He puts in their life. The end of faith as a working measure here is seen in the fact the whole body of Christ is to come into a unity of it. God does everything with a purpose and the Church the body of Christ is no exception to this.

Believers coming into a unity of faith has for many years been all believing in Jesus as the Messiah so that our unity is in fact a fulfillment of this scripture. I say this unity is much more than that, I believe it is a unity of power to be exercised by faith in Christ, not power to only be seen in individual exertions but power to be seen by a corporate effort. An effort made by the whole body of Christ by faith in the power of God.

[14] *That we henceforth be no more children, tossed to and fro, and carried about with every wind of doctrine, by the sleight of men, and cunning craftiness, whereby they lie in wait to deceive;* [15] *But speaking the truth in love, may grow up into him in all things, which is the head, even Christ:* [16] *From whom the whole body fitly joined together and compacted by that which every joint supplieth, according to the effectual working in the measure of every part, maketh increase of the body unto the edifying of itself in love.*

There is a sense of maturity to be seen here founded upon faith in Christ that clearly brings an edification unlike any seen before in the Church's history.

This edification flows out of love, an (Agape) love to be exact that comes only from the presence of the Holy Spirit to be equally dispersed among all its parts.

¹⁷ This I say therefore, and testify in the Lord, that <u>ye henceforth walk not as other Gentiles walk</u>, <u>in the vanity of their mind</u>, ¹⁸ Having the understanding darkened, being alienated from the life of God through the ignorance that is in them, because of the blindness of their heart: ¹⁹ Who being past feeling have given themselves over unto lasciviousness, to work all uncleanness with greediness.

The previous statement is exactly what we see going on in the world and in many churches regarding those who have an emptiness of soul by thinking as the world thinks. They are ignorant of life issues as God sees them because they are blind in heart by spiritual mediocrity that sees no need to be any different and therefore labeled as unclean and without hope. But faith comes from the truth in Christ and is sufficient to be renewed to spiritual thinking that brings forth a new creation as His righteous son or daughter.

²⁰ But ye have not so learned Christ; ²¹ If so be that ye have heard him, and have been taught by him, as <u>the truth is in Jesus</u>: ²² That ye put off concerning the former conversation the old man, which is corrupt according to the deceitful lusts; ²³ And <u>be renewed in the spirit of your mind</u>; ²⁴ And <u>that ye put on the new man</u>, which <u>after God is created in righteousness and true holiness</u>.

Prominence of Faith

CHAPTER EIGHT

Avoid the Spirit of Apathy

If you are in Christ, you have been spiritually removed from the darkness of the kingdoms of this world, and placed into what God says is the kingdom of the Son of His love, qualified and made fit to share the inheritance of all the saints.

Col 1:12-14 ^(AMP) *12 Giving thanks to the Father, Who has qualified and made us fit to share the portion which is the inheritance of the saints (God's holy people) in the Light. 13 [The Father] has delivered and drawn us to Himself out of the control and the dominion of darkness and has transferred us into the kingdom of the Son of His love, 14 In Whom we have our redemption through His blood, [which means] the forgiveness of our sins.*

Nothing here says believers are to have an apathetic posture or that such a position is not the result of a status of mediocrity, but be worthy of the declaration above and know your spiritual heritage is in Christ Jesus.

Eph 6:12-17 ^(NKJV) *For we do not wrestle against flesh and blood, but against principalities, against powers, against the rulers of the darkness of this age, against spiritual hosts of wickedness in the heavenly places.*

All believers are commanded to be engaged in spiritual warfare as laid out in the fact they are given authority and power in the name of Jesus, along with a complete set of spiritual armor, and the sword of the Spirit the word of God.

[13] Wherefore <u>take unto you the whole armour of God</u>, that ye may be able to withstand in the evil day, and having done all, to stand. [14] Stand therefore, having your loins girt about with truth, and having on the breastplate of righteousness; [15] And your feet shod with the preparation of the gospel of peace; [16] Above all, taking the shield of faith, wherewith ye shall be able to quench all the fiery darts of the wicked. [17] And take the helmet of salvation, and <u>the sword of the Spirit, which is the word of God</u>:

You have already seen the enemy's attacks are focused on your destruction, prevention of being free by the word of truth. Jesus says your enemy the devil comes to s*teal*, *kill*, and *destroy* regarding his earthly activity.

John 10:10 *(AMP) The thief comes only in order to **steal** and **kill** and **destroy**. I came that they may have and enjoy life, and have it in abundance (to the full, till it overflows).*

Considering this fact, we will examine these actions or maybe inactions and allow the Holy Spirit to reveal what you need to know concerning how to avoid not only the works of your enemy but how a spirit of apathy comes about and dwells in mediocrity.

Apathy by any definition is a lack of enthusiasm or an initiative to do or be concerned, Today, there are many Christians who have an attitude that reveals no concern about spiritual issues or activities within the Church's. This is seen in the fact there is a lacking in the activity of the Holy Spirit in and among many congregations today which should be alarming, but does not appear to be. Nor the fact the practical teaching and exhortation of the word that grows faith is also in demise.

And yet we have seen how these two things operate at the core of spiritually nurturing His offspring for a fortitude in the spirit, and how without these, a complacency begins to set in. The word steal translated here is (*kleptō*) which means "to steal," and typically is referred to a thief. The devil is the chief thief who comes to steal something not belonging to him. What is it he must he steal?

The word translated kill is (*thyō*) means "to offer up first-fruits to some god;" or to make a sacrifice by slaying a victim, or about killing for a sacrificial purpose. Who or what is he out to kill?

Finally, the word destroy, is (*apollymi*) and means "to utterly destroy;" or "to make perish." However, the idea here is not about extinction, but ruin or loss of the individual's wellbeing. So, how does he ruin one's wellbeing?

Math 13:19 (MSG) *19 When anyone hears news of the kingdom and doesn't take it in, it just remains on the surface, and so the Evil One comes along and plucks it right out of that person's heart. This is the seed the farmer scatters on the road.*

To start with the devil by an act of thievery will steal the word out of someone's heart to prevent the Spirit of God nurturing it to grow and bring faith for a new life in Christ. He knows the purpose of the word and will even go around masquerading as an angel of light to distort any manifestation of it on this earth.

2 Cor 11:14 (AMP) *And it is no wonder, for Satan himself masquerades as an angel of light;*

He influences the foundations of this world so they will have an adverse effect on God's creation. He is bound to material substance of this world working to prevent any truth of the word from being known. And just as He deceived Eve in the garden making her sacrifice the truth God spoke regarding the tree amid the midst of it, the manner of temptation she suffered was in the form of a question.

Gen 3:1-5 *[1] Now the serpent was more subtle than any beast of the field which the LORD God had made. And he said unto the woman, Yea,* <u>*hath God said,*</u> *Ye shall not eat of every tree of the garden? [2] And the woman said unto the serpent, We may eat of the fruit of the trees of the garden: [3] But of the fruit of the tree which is in the midst of the garden,* <u>*God hath said,*</u> <u>*Ye shall not eat of it,*</u> <u>*neither shall ye touch it,*</u> <u>*lest ye die.*</u> *[4] And the serpent said unto the woman,* **<u>Ye shall not surely die</u>***: [5] For God doth know that in the day ye eat thereof, then your eyes shall be opened, and ye shall be as gods, knowing good and evil.*

This question appeared in the form of truth, as he said has not God said, but the question was asked because spiritual ramifications were going to occur based not only on her answer but more so on her actions. If this were not true, then why is the serpent focused on Eve it was Adam who God held accountable.

Eve spoke exactly what God had spoken about eating from the tree in the middle of the garden. But the devil came back that time with a lie saying she would not die, and even though this is not what God said she accepted his deceiving explanation and believed death would not occur if she ate.

So, why is the believer's enemy so focused on keeping them from the truth of the word? It is because God has crafted into it the power needed for it to complete whatever He has spoken for it to do, which if by faith is accepted as truth then no power can stop it.

Isaiah 55:11-13 *[11] So shall my word be that goeth forth out of my mouth: it shall not return unto me void,* <u>*but it shall accomplish*</u> <u>*that which I please,*</u> *and* <u>*it shall prosper in the thing whereto I sent*</u> <u>*it.*</u> *[12] For ye shall go out with joy, and be led forth with peace: the mountains and the hills shall break forth before you into singing, and all the trees of the field shall clap their hands. [13] Instead of the thorn shall come up the fir tree, and instead of the brier shall come* *up the myrtle tree: and it shall be to the LORD for a name, for an everlasting sign that shall not be cut off.*

Believers should take what the word tells them regarding His word doing exactly what He says, since it ends up providing joy, peace, singing, a clapping of hands, and blessing instead of lacking.

It is time for the hills to clap their hands this is going to happen for those who are set free by His word as freedom from the world is so great there will be this supernatural celebration taking place by creation itself.

John 14:10-12 *(MSG) 10 Don't you believe that I am in the Father and the Father is in me? The words that I speak to you aren't mere words. I don't just make them up on my own. The Father who resides in me crafts each word into a divine act. 11 "Believe me: I am in my Father and my Father is in me. If you can't believe that, believe what you see—these works. 12 The person who trusts me will not only do what I'm doing but even greater things, because I, on my way to the Father, am giving you the same work to do that I've been doing. You can count on it.*

Since our enemy focused on keeping us from having in our heart anything revealed from the word, it instructs us to know who brings deliverance from any evil and wickedness that is prevailing.

This is truth we need to know as to why it is important for him to steal the word as quickly as he can before it takes root in one's heart. The next thing Jesus said the enemy does He says he is a <u>killer</u> of maybe something or someone. It is the effectiveness of faith and the word of God as seen in previous chapters he is out to kill.

Math 13:22 *(MSG) 22 "The seed cast in the weeds is the person who hears the kingdom news, but weeds of worry and illusions about getting more and wanting everything under the sun strangle what was heard, and nothing comes of it.*

147

When anyone by the Holy Spirit obtains enough spiritual sense to understand its purpose truth will affect their life, they by faith in it can receive Jesus Christ and become a new creation.

This is something the devil is working to prevent by attempting to *kill* every opportunity for the truth to produce a supernatural transformation of *spirit* and *soul*. He accomplishes this through doubt that arises because of trials or conflicts more in line to the world's ways of doing things but none the less creates doubt that eventually leads to unbelief regarding truth. So the word is strangled of the life it provides.

Gen 3:13 *(AMP)* *And the Lord God said to the woman, What is this you have done? And the woman said, The serpent beguiled (cheated, outwitted, and deceived) me, and I ate.*

Notice something in the above verse, here a child of the creation Eve, is outwitted, and deceived by her enemy the devil. This same thing continues to occur today because of deceptions by the same enemy through pulpits who do not have ability to know if he is talking them out of telling the truth and abandoning what they have heard from the Spirit of God for a more worldly affect.

His deceptive words keep many from holding up the truth that allows the Spirit of God to nurture His offspring. There is revelation shown here, in that Adam and Eve had no worldly influences occurring during this event as the world as we know it was not yet present. They had only known the glory of God and the presence of the Holy Spirit, thus the ability of the enemy to deceive a believer is not based on the world but on truths they do not yet know.

So, it is very important believers learn to perceive not only what the enemy is doing but how it keeps them from any knowledge and understanding of truth from the word. If we continue with this, we must look at the third thing Jesus said the enemy has come to do, he has also come to destroy.

The thing he must destroy is faith for spiritual growth, as this is something God purposely crafts into His word so that what is to occur happens as planned. Here the enemy works to influence everything in a believer's life, career, finances, spouses, family, friends, ministry, and spiritual areas of the body of Christ.

Math 13:24-30 (MSG) *24 He told another story. "God's kingdom is like a farmer who planted good seed in his field. 25 That night, while his hired men were asleep, his enemy sowed thistles all through the wheat and slipped away before dawn. 26 When the first green shoots appeared and the grain began to form, the thistles showed up, too. 27 "The farmhands came to the farmer and said, 'Master, that was clean seed you planted, wasn't it? Where did these thistles come from?' 28 "He answered, 'Some enemy did this.' "The farmhands asked, 'Should we weed out the thistles?' 29 "He said, 'No, if you weed the thistles, you'll pull up the wheat, too. 30 Let them grow together until harvest time. Then I'll instruct the harvesters to pull up the thistles and tie them in bundles for the fire, then gather the wheat and put it in the barn.' "*

Many have lost their focus of faith and ceased to grow simply because they see the world's way as an easier means to obtain a more secure and prosperous position. The reason for a spirit of apathy from all of this is to effectively get Christians to accept mediocrity and rest in the worlds system of doing things.

Once believers are there the authority and power of the word no longer affects their life or the life of another. But despite the thistle that grows alongside the wheat there are many still growing by the word and the Spirit.

Rom 12:2 (MSG) *Don't become like the people of this world. Instead, change the way you think. Then you will always be able to determine what God really wants—what is good, pleasing, and perfect.*

Ending up in situations and circumstances contrary to the will of God, convinced in your mind and heart it is easier to live life by the systems of this world than by the word of God, is dangerous.

1 John 2:16 *(NKJ)* *For* *all that is in the world--the lust of the flesh, the lust of the eyes, and the pride of life--is not of the Father but is of the world.*

The enemy is out to destroy the ability of the word to set us free of sin and poverty and nourishing and maintaining of our spiritual wellbeing of *spirit* and *soul*, so that when believers attempt to reveal an image of God, it is out of character to Him.

Some of you think the enemy cannot do any of this, and all you must do is believe and everything will be all right. Your right you do not have to believe any of this or live by a nature having any spiritual sense about your life. He will not force you to do so, but allows you to do whatever you want, live however you want, and be whoever you want, it is your will influencing your life do what you want. God even allows you to go to hell if that is what you will to do, but I tell you it is not what He wills for your life.

The blessings of God cover every aspect of your life *spirit*, *soul*, and *body* able to fulfill what God says on the earth. But it requires *a believer* having spiritual sense to know they exist and perceive how they are to be used by them.

Apathy vs Blessings

Math 13:23 *(GW)* *And the seed which was put in good earth, this is* *he who gives ear to the word,* *and* *gets the sense of it;* *who gives fruit, some a hundred, some sixty, some thirty times as much.*

The condition of a person's heart makes the difference between those on the wayside, and those called good ground. Good ground here is the heart that is right before God.

This requires a nature that operates by sensible spiritual principles regarding blessings all of which has to do with spiritual wellbeing. The key element here being spiritual, or (***pneumatikos***), the idea of something invisible having supernatural prominence.

1 Cor 2:13 *(GWD)* *We don't speak about these things using teachings that are based on intellectual arguments like people do. Instead, <u>we use the Spirit's teachings</u>. We <u>explain spiritual things to those who have the Spirit</u>.*

Everything on earth has origin from God and is by His nature to be in harmony with the spiritual character of all creation. The devil is at work deforming God's character in creation, by creating spiritual activity through principalities, powers, rulers of darkness, and spiritual wickedness in high places. This brings about a warfare that as scripture says every offspring of God is to be engaged in not against flesh and blood but against forces of wickedness and evil.

God says the whole company or His family the Church, are a spiritual house where spiritual sacrifices are offered by those who believe in Christ. And it is the word of God that is spiritual seed to produce blessings to be seen in our living as a child of God, and not natural to the ways of the world.

These blessings sustain your spiritual wellbeing while here as His son or daughter, He insures He will provide whatever needed for a whole being of *spirit*, *soul*, and *body*.

1 Peter 2:5 *(GW)* *You come to him as <u>living stones</u>, a <u>spiritual house</u> that is being built into a <u>holy priesthood</u>. So offer spiritual sacrifices that God accepts through Jesus Christ.*

The enemy uses a spirit of apathy to promote mediocrity among believers stalling or preventing them from making those spiritual sacrifices or a better translation would be spiritual offerings to God by a consciousness to the things of God.

So, believers need to look at this from God's perspective, they are citizens of a spiritual kingdom, children of a royal family, hierarchs in His theocracy of government, carriers of His kingdom, equipped to operate supernatural gifts, and have a spiritual ability founded upon His constitution of righteousness.

However, pulpits using worldly systems in conflict with all this allows the enemy to combat believers by a wicked spiritual culture of evil. But the word reveals God will do abundantly above all we can ever expect or even imagine by a power that works in us by the Holy Spirit. This should be all we need to know as a child of God, since there is no greater power than this on earth and it operates only through those, He calls His offspring.

Eph 3:20 Now unto him that is able to do exceeding abundantly above all that we ask or think, <u>according to the power that worketh in us</u>.

When we talk about spiritual blessings, we are talking about those things sourced and operated under the authority and power of God. Worldly blessings operate by a cursed economic system under an influence of our enemy the devil. Spiritual blessings are by God expressly given to those who are His, and operate by a supernatural power.

Something believers must discern is that the power of the Holy Spirit is to work in and through each blessing the whole person for having wealth, riches, or material substance described in the word as for confirmation of covenant. This is something purposed not to establish His kingdom in us on earth but maintain us while here for 2000 years of the Church age.

Deut 8:18 ¹⁸ But thou shalt remember the LORD thy God: for it is he that giveth thee power to get wealth, <u>that he may establish his covenant which he sware unto thy fathers</u>, as it is this day.

If we look at blessings in considering wealth, we see they are brought into manifestation by faith in the word of God, designed to fulfill His will in our life and through our life to those who are in need.

However, one's spiritual wellbeing is not based on riches of money or any wealth of material goods, it is based on whether they operate by the principles God has applied to His blessings. The one thing believers must know is all blessings still belong to God, and they are mere stewards of them while here on this earth.

Luke 12:42 And the Lord said, Who then is that faithful and wise steward, whom his lord shall make ruler over his household, to give them their portion of meat in due season?

To be a good steward is to know that in sight of the one who gives blessings means your stewardship is going to deal with many substances that are not natural but are spiritual and supernaturally empowered.

³ Then the steward said within himself, What shall I do? for my lord taketh away from me the stewardship: I cannot dig; to beg I am ashamed.

Truths pertaining to this stewardship or oversight of blessings reveals accountability goes right along with a responsibility of what it is, an appointed position by God. The problem with apathy is it builds up a disregard and promotes non-conformance to knowledge of how believers are to do what God holds them responsible for.

This steward was obviously doing his job, but either stopped or changed something and came under judgment. I could say blessings are everything when it comes to one being a good steward of the master's goods. But when one is apathetic to the responsibility of it, they have no distribution of them occurring, and will be positioned for correction and/or rebuke by the Holy Spirit.

[4] Ah, <u>I've got a plan</u>. Here's what I'll do... then when I'm turned out into the street, people will take me into their houses.' [5] Then he went at it. One after another, he called in the people who were in debt to his master. He said to the first, 'How much do you owe my master?' [6] "He replied, 'A hundred jugs of olive oil.' "The manager said, 'Here, take your bill, sit down here quick now write fifty.' [7] "To the next he said, 'And you, what do you owe?' "He answered, 'A hundred sacks of wheat.' "He said, 'Take your bill, write in eighty.'

If this steward had continued to operate the spiritual blessings of the kingdom in a way common to such responsibility, he would still have his stewardship. And as we see in this message format, the steward did what many today do he laid down his accountability to God and turned to the world and its ways. Yet he still tied to live as a child of God, but stewardship is not about how to survive the needs the world, it is about being a steward of your master's blessings.

[8] "Now here's a surprise: <u>The master praised the crooked manager</u>! And why? Because <u>he knew how to look after himself</u>. Streetwise people are smarter in this regard than law-abiding citizens. They are on constant alert, looking for angles, surviving by their wits.

He even received praise from his master because of his wisely positioning himself to be acceptable to those living according to the systems of the world. What is strange though, if He had used the same enthusiasm and intent, he garnered in seeing how the world and its systems operate, he could have done the same for his master. And would not be in this situation.

[9] <u>I want you to be smart in the same way</u>—<u>but for what is right</u>— using every adversity to stimulate you to creative survival, to concentrate your attention on the bare essentials, so you'll live, really live, and not complacently just get by on good behavior."

154

When believers fail to live according to principles of blessings, they are being received and welcomed into another kingdom, the kingdom of this world. Where they will find themselves bound by an evil spirit of economics.

Meaning if one uses blessings of God to try and establish or maintain some natural stability while sowing them into systems of this world without any direction of the Holy Spirit. It will be unfruitful because the power of it is limited to and secured in an evil Babylonian system having no power over it.

To sustain a believer's spiritual wellbeing or the wellbeing of others because of the wickedness active in the economics that abide they end up finding their place of habitation is no longer founded upon the systems of God but on the world's way of doing business. Which to someone apathetic there are no spiritual principles to be honorably accountable for.

[10] *Jesus went on to make these comments: <u>If you're honest in small things, you'll be honest in big things;</u> [11] If you're a crook in small things, you'll be a crook in big things.[12] If you're not honest in small jobs, who will put you in charge of the store?*

I want us to focus on a fact here, in that when believers do not do well with a worldly substance such as money then how can God trust them with true riches of supernaturally empowered spiritual blessings. Stewardship is a responsibility to be attentive to what the Holy Spirit instructs you to do, so that God's will be done, not the will of the banks, or politicians, or governmental agencies.

[13] *<u>No worker can serve two bosses</u>: He'll either hate the first and love the second Or adore the first and despise the second. You can't serve both God and the Bank.*

Apathy running through the Church is founded upon an intent to do everything out of anxiety or anxiousness as the world does.

God in no way desires to place any believer into a failed stewardship for the sake of gaining recognition in the world, nor use them as some disposable asset to accomplish a spiritual prowess. It is all about overseeing the blessings that brings giving birth to more spiritual offspring.

You as a believer in Christ may have messed up and the devil has taken your stuff and hindered your ability to produce spiritual fruit, most especially your gifts and callings of ministry. But the God who made you to be His son or daughter has more than enough to see to your restoration and replenishment again, and again.

Thus, anything a believer has lost to this worlds system or to some activity of the enemy is still available and He is willing to provide it. Because you are established in the eternal promises of God, promises that He cannot break or else He would not be who He is. Thus, He does all the things that are impossible for you so you need to take heart in the fact He has blessed you and will bless you to be a blessing in this world. Amen.

A Little Sleep a Little Slumber and here comes Apathy.

Prov 24:30-34 *[30] I went by the field of the <u>slothful</u>, and by the vineyard of the man <u>void of understanding</u>; [31] And, lo, it was all grown over with thorns, and nettles had covered the face thereof, and the stone wall thereof was broken down. [32] Then I saw, and considered it well: I looked upon it, and received instruction. [33] Yet a little sleep, a little slumber, a little folding of the hands to sleep: [34] <u>So shall thy poverty come as one that travelleth</u>; and thy want as an armed man.*

The power such blessings will not benefit you or God if you end up in poverty based on the wealth and riches of this world, and not on the condition of one's *spirit* and *soul*. The devil has no right to a believer's stuff, he is defeated, and he has no authority over anything here.

But if an ignorance or choosing to do stupidly pertaining to them is present then he can interrupt the process of blessings God has purposed to enter in this earth empowered to do His will.

Apathy breeds a slothfulness to the things of God and stops the supernatural work of the word in one's life causing a dormant faith ineffective in doing God's will. And though the previous scripture outlines the results of not taking care of one's natural source of wellbeing I believe it is the same in the spiritual perspective. If we fail to nurture our *spirit* and *soul* by the word of God along with fellowship of the Spirit, then we become poverty ridden spiritually.

Rev 3:14-19 *14 And unto the angel of the church of the Laodiceans write; These things saith the Amen, the faithful and true witness, the beginning of the creation of God; 15 I know thy works, that thou art neither cold nor hot: I would thou wert cold or hot. 16 So then because thou art lukewarm, and neither cold nor hot, I will spue thee out of my mouth.*

The spiritual condition of the church at Laodicea is exactly what we are talking about, spiritual mediocrity here is an apathetic status the Lord is unwilling to accept. Because of a condition He says is lukewarm, meaning any work of ministry is neither hot nor cold as result He will spew them out of His mouth.

Anyone minded seeing themselves as sufficient in all things of God are also lent to apathy as they see themselves not in need of anymore increase of anything for spiritual maturity.

17 Because thou sayest, I am rich, and increased with goods, and have need of nothing; and knowest not that thou art wretched, and miserable, and poor, and blind, and naked:

Wretched as stated here is describing one who is miserable and in a poor state of *spirit,* blind to truth, and uncovered or is exposed to evil elements around them.

Elements that could be formed by spiritual forces not of God, seeking destruction of not only their individual life, but in this case, the spirit life of a Church. No matter what status we are in spiritually the Lord still desires to save us from all iniquity whether self-made or of the enemy. It is His counsel of righteousness that brings one to a wealth and riches that only He can provide.

[18] I counsel thee to buy of me gold tried in the fire, that thou mayest be rich; and white raiment, that thou mayest be clothed, and that the shame of thy nakedness do not appear; and anoint thine eyes with eyesalve, that thou mayest see. [19] <u>As many as I love</u>, <u>I rebuke and chasten</u>: be zealous therefore, and repent.

All believers have a covenant that decrees they prosper in every aspect of life. Thus, He will never give up on them, but they can give up on Him through apathetic attitudes that see no need to do as He commands.

Math 10:32-33 *[32] Whosoever therefore shall confess me before men, him will I confess also before my Father which is in heaven. [33] But <u>whosoever shall deny me before men</u>, <u>him will I also deny before my Father which is in heaven.</u>*

For a believer it is spiritually dangerous to lose sight of the fact there are things going on caused by the devil or church or peers or the world designed to encourage them to become mediocre in a life in Christ. But diligence to keep oneself nurtured and fervent in the things of God to what He holds them accountable to do comes only by truths that bolds they are free to be exercisers of an authority and power established in Christ.

CHAPTER NINE
Transformed – Spiritually.

The offspring of the Mighty God we call Abba Father, have all been given a spiritual dominion in this world to reveal His will, and the glory of Jesus Christ His Son. We are here to manifest a kingdom on earth that reveals His presence in us and through us, by the Holy Spirit. Our lives are to characterize our spiritual Father just like Jesus revealed Him by His Spirit assisted life in the flesh. And as a son or daughter of God the Holy Spirit has shown us that we have available to us all manner of spiritual blessings established in Christ Jesus before the foundations of this earth were created.

Eph 1:3-4 Blessed be the God and Father of our Lord Jesus Christ, who hath blessed us with all spiritual blessings in heavenly places in Christ: ⁴ According as he hath chosen us in him before the foundation of the world, that we should be holy and without blame before him in love:

These blessings are for fulfilling the intent and concern in the heart of our heavenly Father, they come from Him and every one of them is established in Christ Jesus. And since He paid the price for them there is nothing, we can do to earn them they are freely given to anyone who receives Him.

Transformed – Spiritually.

As we saw in the previous chapters such blessings are important to God for His will being done through us on this earth. So, as sons and daughters we have a spiritual heritage that is laid out in Jesus Christ, that requires us to live our lives according to the power of the Spirit of God.

Rom 8:12-14 Therefore, brethren, we are debtors--not to the flesh, to live according to the flesh. [13] For if you live according to the flesh you will die; but if by the Spirit you put to death the deeds of the body, you will live. [14] For as many as are led by the Spirit of God, these are sons of God.

For one to be led by the Spirit of God they must be willing to be observant of what the Lord reveals and obedient to do it. Many think that being led by Him is just doing whatever they see in scripture as a ministerial debut, but that is not what the above verse means. It means to have a spiritual sense that knows what is and what is not of the Holy Spirit. You might be surprised if you knew how many people blaspheme the Holy Spirit simply because they have no idea what it means.

Mark 3:28-29 (AMP) [28] Truly and solemnly I say to you, all sins will be forgiven the sons of men, and whatever abusive and blasphemous things they utter; [29] But whoever speaks abusively against or maliciously misrepresents the Holy Spirit can never get forgiveness, but is guilty of and is in the grasp of an everlasting trespass.

We need to put this in perspective so we will know what Jesus was talking about which has all to do with religious leaders calling the one working through Him casting out devils, an unclean spirit.

Mark 3:22-23 [22] And the scribes which came down from Jerusalem said, He hath Beelzebub, and by the prince of the devils casteth he out devils. [23] And he called them unto him, and said unto them in parables, How can Satan cast out Satan?

Beelzebub is another name for Satan, so in other words these religious leaders were calling the Holy Spirit who was working through Jesus in casting out demons and delivering people from demonic torment, Satan. They were so fearful of the power that worked through Him they believed it had to come from the devil himself. I want you to see they did not call Jesus Satan they called the one in Him Satan.

Therefore, Jesus made the statement of calling the Holy Spirit an unclean spirit is a blasphemous event that among all blasphemous events cannot be removed. This means those priests will be required to give an account of what they said when they appear before Christ, and no repentance will be accepted for it. There are many in the body of Christ who have committed this same mistake because they were unlearned in how the Holy Spirit operates among God's offspring.

Rev 20:11-12 [11] *And I saw a great white throne, and him that sat on it, from whose face the earth and the heaven fled away; and there was found no place for them.* [12] *And I saw the dead, small and great, stand before God; and the books were opened: and another book was opened, which is the book of life: and the dead were judged out of those things which were written in the books, according to their works.*

Rom 14:10-12 [10] *But why dost thou judge thy brother? or why dost thou set at nought thy brother? for we shall all stand before the judgment seat of Christ.* [11] *For it is written, As I live, saith the Lord, every knee shall bow to me, and every tongue shall confess to God.* [12] *So then every one of us shall give account of himself to God.*

The Holy Spirit's presence with and in us is God's own personal guarantee of His eternal investment in revealing to every believer that His work of supernatural manifestations is by an inheritance in, Jesus Christ. Any lack of an understanding this is relevant to one's immaturity.

Transformed – Spiritually.

Eph 1:13-14 In Him you also trusted, after you heard the word of truth, the gospel of your salvation; in whom also, having believed, you were <u>sealed with the Holy Spirit of promise,</u>

You are seen by God as worth the price Jesus paid for your sins in redeeming you from the law of sin and death. And the fact is the Holy Spirit is the one purposely guaranteeing your inheritance until you arrive in the eternal presence of your Father God.

¹⁴ <u>who is the guarantee of our inheritance until the redemption of the purchased possession,</u> to the praise of His glory.

God's testimony of blessing is confirmed in His word through Jesus Christ birth, life, death, and resurrection, so it is important we see ourselves as He sees us, obedient of His Son Jesus Christ.

Rom 8:16-17 The <u>Spirit itself beareth witness with our spirit, that we are the children of God:</u> ¹⁷ And if children, then heirs; heirs of God, and joint-heirs with Christ; if so be that we suffer with him, that we may be also glorified together.

A Dominion of Blessing

The biggest issue most believers have in seeing themselves with this dominion is they do not have knowledge and understanding of who they really are. As most just see themselves as a Christian who believes in Jesus Christ the Son of God. While this is true, they fail in having a spiritual perception of who or what a person who calls themselves a child of God is according to His interpretation.

Gen 1:26-28 And God said, Let us make man in our image, after our likeness: and <u>let them have dominion</u> over the fish of the sea, and over the fowl of the air, and over the cattle, and over all the earth, and over every creeping thing that creepeth upon the earth.

All of humanity is destined for an image of God appearance but not all will be workers of it in the manner He has ordained in Christ Jesus.

Those who know and understand who they are in Christ have been placed into this authority not by anything they have done but by covenant with God. His commandment to replenish an earth, is with humanity represented by two sexes one being male and the other being female.

²⁷ So God created man in his own image, in the image of God created he him; male and female created he them. ²⁸ And God blessed them, and God said unto them, Be fruitful, and multiply, and replenish the earth, and subdue it: and <u>have dominion</u> over the fish of the sea, and over the fowl of the air, and over every living thing that moveth upon the earth.

Both as believers are blessed to be God's blessing in this earth, and are to be willing and obedient to do as the Holy Spirit leads them in their working out their salvation in Christ with understanding of what God's intent, and concern is. Neither is above the other both have equal status in this hierarchy, but if married an additional statute is in place because marriage has an ordained covering of headship to be wholly accepted by Him.

Eph 5:21-25 *²¹ Submitting yourselves one to another in the fear of God. ²² Wives, <u>submit yourselves unto your own husbands, as unto the Lord</u>. ²³ For <u>the husband is the head of the wife</u>, even as <u>Christ is the head of the church</u>: and he is the saviour of the body.*

In both cases above headship is a spiritual position ordained by God. Dominion is seen by many as a dominance of sorts and not as one positioned within the hierarchy of God's government. But He has established a system of blessing built upon righteousness that incorporates several elements or individuals be involved. And it is all orchestrated by God, overseen by Jesus His Son, and carried out by the Holy Spirit through those who are led by Him. He loves His creation of males and females enough to see to it every need is met in the life He intended for them.

Transformed – Spiritually.

John 3:2 ^(AMP) *But <u>he who practices truth</u> [who does what is right] <u>comes out into the Light</u>; so that his works may be plainly shown to be what they are—wrought with God [divinely prompted, done with God's help, in dependence upon Him].*

Everything God promised is tied to this system of blessing, so we must learn how to bring into manifestation in our lives every portion of it by faith in His ability. This dominion is a position of authority God put in place through which these blessings flow. And as we see there are individuals and events that must all align to the will of the Father so that it is being done as He purposed.

Luke 12:31-34 ^(GW) *Steep yourself in <u>God-reality, God-initiative, God-provisions</u>. You'll find all your everyday human concerns will be met. ³² Don't be afraid of missing out. You're my dearest friends! <u>The Father wants to give you the very kingdom itself</u>.*

As in the case of marriage where there is an applied headship to the husband it is not for ruling the wife but for alignment to the flow of blessings God intends upon providing. All for the purpose of His will being done in the process of procreation and spiritual growth and development of His offspring. Authority has a path it must flow through to maintain any power associated to it, in this case a power that is built upon righteousness.

The activity of God, Jesus, and the Holy Spirit are not who He says are to be in dominion, believers are the ones this refers to, since He said *"let them have dominion"* over all creation. In the beginning this was not the case as before Adam fell all humanity was deemed to be the ones in dominion here. This puts great emphasis on the part of believers flowing blessings into this earth. And since all the Godhead agrees on this, becoming transformed spiritually to operate by dominion and authority in a manner described is important.

Now do not get all wound up over you having dominion and authority that in your thinking allows you to wield a prowess of self-rulership. This dominion is never effective in having authority over any part of humanity, as no one has the right to rule over a person's will. And it has nothing to do with wielding power on earth, but has everything to do with power by His authority through a dominion, to bless those aligned in creation.

God has a kingdom in heaven, but the very presence of His character is to be in all who are born again evident in the fact this kingdom is within them. Not in a physical sense, but in a spiritual one that is seen through an interaction with the Holy Spirit doing as the ruler of the kingdom wills to do. Having principles that must be applied, but require spiritual sense to discern.

Luke 17:20-21 [20] *And when he was demanded of the Pharisees, when the kingdom of God should come, he answered them and said, The kingdom of God cometh not with observation:* [21] *Neither shall they say, Lo here! or, lo there! for, behold, the kingdom of God is within you.*

Something we should have consciousness of is that dominion is not an option, I mean God did not say let them have dominion if they want to, but in verse 27 He reiterates they are to have dominion, a commandment for us to fulfill exactly what He says.

The unknown aspect of an authority that is to be exercised on earth that is from a creator God by such a dominion, is there are no powers or authorities greater. And why believers are to know and understand what it is all about so blessings He intends to promote into the earth are freely flowing because of their transformation, spiritually. We state faith comes by hearing and hearing by the word of God, but I believe this is more directly related to knowledge and understanding of things as revealed in the word by the Holy Spirit.

Transformed – Spiritually.

How To Be Transformed

As God by faith perceived us serving Him, ourselves, and others as He purposed mediocrity was not a part of it because it does not accept this as spiritual truth.

Rom 10:17 ^(MSG) *The point is, Before you trust, you have to listen. But <u>unless Christ's Word is preached, there's nothing to listen to</u>.*

Again apply spiritual sense here regarding faith and include your spiritual heritage. I believe herein lies a key for the child of God, in that God already loves you and desires to bless you continually in your life. Therefore, faith is not required to get from God blessings He by His love has already positioned to give you.

Ps 68:19 *Blessed be the Lord, <u>who daily loadeth us with benefits</u>, even the God of our salvation. Selah.*

I know that cuts across all the traditional teaching regarding faith, but let us allow the Holy Spirit to teach us something here. I believe God is not expecting us to constantly use faith to get what He already said He lovingly desires to give us, but He gave us faith to use to get what is present in a supernatural realm into the earth.

Phil 4:19 ^(MSG) *You can be sure that God will take care of everything you need, his generosity exceeding even yours in the glory that pours from Jesus.*

Let me emphasis, what He is requiring of us is to live by faith in Jesus Christ, so that through the knowledge and understanding of truth as revealed by the Holy Spirit we willingly exercise authority for His purpose. He expects us to serve Him not denominations, or organizations, or dynamic ministries to reveal the unseen kingdom into this earth, bringing manifestation to all supernatural blessings which are not naturally possible.

However, in your servitude to Him you may fulfill positions in these various areas. But the intent in His heart whatever you do to serve is based on faith in His working in and through you.

Math 14:28-31 And Peter answered Him, Lord, if it is You, command me to come to You on the water. ²⁹ He said, Come! So Peter got out of the boat and walked on the water, and he came toward Jesus.

Peter walked on water, manifesting in the natural a supernatural event, and no one outside of Christ has ever, or even today, walked on water. In that moment, his faith made a supernatural thing occur in the presence of the disciples not natural to the working of things on the earth, an otherwise supernaturally possible event.

Math 15:22-28 ^(NKJV) And behold, a woman of Canaan came from that region and cried out to Him, saying, "Have mercy on me, O Lord, Son of David! My daughter is severely demon-possessed." ²³ But He answered her not a word. And His disciples came and urged Him, saying, "Send her away, for she cries out after us." ²⁴ But He answered and said, "I was not sent except to the lost sheep of the house of Israel." ²⁵ Then she came and worshiped Him, saying, "Lord, help me!" ²⁶ But He answered and said, "It is not good to take the children's bread and throw it to the little dogs." ²⁷ And she said, "Yes, Lord, yet even the little dogs eat the crumbs which fall from their masters' table."

This woman a Canaanite who is also a gentile from Palestine, was not a disciple of Christ, yet we see in this event her faith was serving her, and brought about something that in the natural was impossible. While we typically do not view healing as significant as one walking on water, it still required her faith to happen.

²⁸ Then Jesus answered and said to her, "O woman, great is your faith! Let it be to you as you desire." And her daughter was healed from that very hour.

While faith may be about quantity it is also about quality, in that one's faith verses another's faith is not solely about how much one has, but about how much one uses faith to serve God. In Peter's case, Jesus said, oh you of *little faith,* but in the case of the Canaanite woman He said woman *great is your faith*. What made a difference?

Faith as seen by Jesus was not about who the individual is, but about how they used it, as both believed in Jesus's ability, and each used faith to bring something into the natural that did not yet exist. Peter had faith for a moment, but it was not to the degree of the Canaanite woman's evident in the fact it served him until fear and doubt appeared. But her faith was considered great because she did not allow fear and doubt to intervene concerning who she was.

Mark 11:23-24 [23] *For verily I say unto you, That whosoever shall say unto this mountain, Be thou removed, and be thou cast into the sea; and shall not doubt in his heart, but shall believe that those things which he saith shall come to pass; he shall have whatsoever he saith.* [24] *Therefore I say unto you, What things soever ye desire, when ye pray, believe that ye receive them, and ye shall have them.*

A certain principle is at work here, personal faith brings into manifestation something from an unseen realm that has no bearing on whether it is for throwing mulberry trees into the sea, moving mountains, or bringing forth healing, or even one walking on water. What is relevant to knowing and understanding is the main process to be applied to breach any realm of doubt, is un-mediocre-d Faith.

Math 9:27-30 *And when Jesus went on from there, two blind men came after him, crying out, Have mercy on us, you Son of David.* [28] *And when he had come into the house, the blind men came to him; and Jesus said to them, Have you faith that I am able to do this? They said to him, Yes, Lord.* [29] *Then he put his hand on their eyes, saying, As your faith is, let it be done to you.*

Jesus asked these two blind men if their faith can receive His ability, and they said yes, and it was done. Jesus had great faith, and we see how He used His faith to serve His Father and creation while here in the flesh.

30 And their eyes were made open. And Jesus said to them sharply, Let no man have knowledge of it.

He constantly brought supernatural power through signs, wonders, and miracles into this natural realm. As we continue to view the word to spiritually transform, we are receiving by the Holy Spirit truths concerning all the things God has declared for us and enlarging our habitation on earth. Faith equips believers with a spiritual ability to do what cannot be done naturally.

His faith working in His life brought into the earth those things that were supernatural, exposing His Father's will. Our faith works according to what we believe, and will never serve us in greater things unless we dare to trust God who is always able to do what is impossible.

Faith is given to us to bring into manifestation all things God has decreed to His creation. And not for us to do as we will, but do His will in bringing the kingdom to light in this world through Jesus Christ His Son.

Every believer must get hold of transformation truths revealed in God's word, for faithfully operating as His spiritual offspring, by a nature that uses faith to do just as He would do.

There is another aspect of faith that we need to understand, and the Apostle Paul is bringing it to the for-front by revealing God is working in His creation to bring spiritual transformation. As we will see in these scriptures Gentiles were not part of the Church in the beginning, Jesus began with Jewish Israel, who prophetically were to receive foundations of spiritual principles for Christ Church.

Transformed – Spiritually.

Rom 11:17-24 ^(MSG) *Some of the tree's branches were pruned and you wild olive shoots were grafted in. Yet the fact that you are now fed by that rich and holy root* ¹⁸ *gives you no cause to crow over the pruned branches. Remember, you aren't feeding the root;* <u>*the root is feeding you*</u>*.*

Paul says those branches from a wild olive tree were Gentiles, willing to be of the nature and purpose of the Church, they have been grafted into a recently pruned olive tree, who was Israel. The results of the Lord removing unbelieving Israel from its spiritual purpose not the Church, was grafting in those who were not of the heritage of Israel. This was done because they by faith were willing to receive the truths to transform into God's spiritual offspring fulfilling His will as the Church on earth.

¹⁹ *It's certainly possible to say, "Other branches were pruned so that I could be grafted in!"* ²⁰ *Well and good. But they were pruned because they were deadwood, no longer connected by belief and commitment to the root.* <u>*The only reason you're on the tree is because your graft "took" when you believed, and because you're connected to that belief-nurturing root*</u>*. So don't get cocky and strut your branch. Be humbly mindful of the root that keeps you lithe and green.*

This reverse aspect of faith is unbelief, which as we see here was contrary in nature to the root that supplied the branches. This root he talks about here is Christ the anointed Messiah. Israel was cut off from this root because of unbelief and new branches, the Gentiles were grafted into it.

Something you need to understand the new branches will not change the tree's spiritual purpose what it is to be by the nature of the SAP (spiritual nourishment) being supplied by Christ, is still the same as before Israel was cut off. One of the great apostasies is man taking control of Christ Church.

²¹ If God didn't think twice about taking pruning shears to the natural branches, why would he hesitate over you? He wouldn't give it a second thought.

All branches are to be of the same nature as the root so that the purpose of the olive tree, in this case working through the body of Christ His Church, is fulfilled. Unbelief cuts off the nurturing source of the Holy Spirit, and any dead branches unable to produce spiritual fruit are going to be cut off. This is a serious matter to God, anyone who is without such a nature is in doubt and just as they were before, spiritually dead un-transformed creations.

²³ And don't get to feeling superior to those pruned branches down on the ground. If they don't persist in remaining deadwood, they could very well get grafted back in. God can do that. He can perform miracle grafts.

Things written here are to provoke you into seeing God has an eternal purpose for all associated to the truth revealed through Christ interaction with us. Those of Israel who come to believe in Jesus as the Christ, the Messiah, are all afforded the same work of spiritual transformation every believer receives, because they are established by faith in the same truths to bring knowledge and understanding.

²⁴ Why, if he could graft you—branches cut from a tree out in the wild—into an orchard tree, he certainly isn't going to have any trouble grafting branches back into the tree they grew from in the first place. Just be glad you're in the tree, and hope for the best for the others.

There is one thing I know above all, and that is that God does not change, what He by faith has purposed before the foundations of this earth are still purposed for the same results by our faith today. I am convinced He will bring all of it together in the ending days of the Church but for now we are to be about becoming exactly what he says we are.

Transformed – Spiritually.

Transforming a Family

Now my brothers and sisters in Christ, or my spiritual siblings, I want you to know that by your love toward me you are to influence and provoke me to good works, and to live a right standing life in relationship toward all especially every part of the family of God.

Heb 10:24-25 ^(AMP) *And let us consider and give attentive, continuous care to watching over one another, studying how we may stir up (stimulate and incite) to love and helpful deeds and noble activities,* ²⁵ *Not forsaking or neglecting to assemble together [as believers], as is the habit of some people, but admonishing (warning, urging, and encouraging) one another, and all the more faithfully as you see the day approaching.*

Anyone who is a son or daughter of God should already know it is important for them to come together to stimulate love for one another, and help one another by giving attention to the life each is living.

Phil 1:9-11 ⁹ *And this I pray, that your love may abound yet more and more in knowledge and in all judgment;* ¹⁰ *That ye may approve things that are excellent; that ye may be sincere and without offence till the day of Christ;* ¹¹ *Being filled with the fruits of righteousness, which are by Jesus Christ, unto the glory and praise of God.*

All believers in Christ are as spiritual sibling without offense of one another influencing each other's lives as a child of God through fellowship in the Holy Spirit by a Divine nature. Those in Christ, are the only ones by whom He brings into this world supernatural signs, wonders, and miracles by a faithfulness to Him as already seen. And these same believers are to be speaking warnings, with urgings or encouragements to one another, always looking toward the day of their savior's return. They must be all about having the same intent and concern in their hearts as the Father has in His for His creation.

However, the fact remains among believer's true knowledge and instruction on how to have sibling interaction with one another by the Holy Spirit is severely immature and lacking in bringing about spiritual transformations. Lest you forget everything that goes on in a marriage covenant, a personal relationship, or family and church environments, effects your spiritual wellbeing. And in turn effects the overall spiritual health and wellbeing of the body of believers you associate with.

My revealing that fellowship among believers is to be a spiritual event by the Holy Spirit is so you and I as a living part of the body are actively aligned to the will of our heavenly Father. But because of the various denominations and religious sects there is a schism present over fellowship making such a manifestation never at the forefront of any gatherings.

What little has occurred is becoming something of the past, as today it is seen as no longer necessary among local church pulpits resulting in a now presence of mediocre-d unity. An expected fact when today believer's interest and focus is more on things like social media, interactive events that convey no spiritual nurturing.

God told me something a long time ago, only His sheep produce more sheep by revelation truth of the word, as sheep replenishment occurs by ministry and fellowship. Imagine how many believers would be in the churches if all in Christ were working as a unified fellowship.

So, for those who are His child, there must be a picture formed in your spiritual consciousness that constantly reveals by the Holy Spirit, what should appear regarding you, as you by faith transform into whom you are to be according to His will.

2 Cor 6:14-18 *(AMP)* *14 Do not be unequally yoked with unbelievers [do not make mis-mated alliances with them or come under a different yoke with them, inconsistent with your faith]. For what partnership have right living and right standing with God with iniquity and lawlessness? Or how can light have fellowship with darkness?*

Paul makes a good point here your fellowship must be aligned with others who are of like character or better said are living by a right standing in Christ rather than standing in lawlessness of sin and iniquity in the world.

Nowadays many churches are pandering to the masses to get people's attention all for recognition from ministerial peers. This breeds spiritually unfamiliar kinds of believers among the flock as many are there just because they are treated exactly how they want to be as a so-called sheep of God.

However, let anything get out of line to their expectations and they will by a spirit of hatefulness bring a discontentment among the congregation.

[15] What harmony can there be between Christ and Belial [the devil]? Or what has a believer in common with an unbeliever?

It has always been an issue for discussion in the Church when a question about allowing unbelievers to attend services comes up. Most accept them and hope they eventually get saved and become a member. Not to say this is not OK, as it is better for them to be among a group of believers than a group of unbelievers.

But today that thinking is pre-mandating a strong resistance to truths from scripture that speak to a righteous manner of life by a congregation of believers.

[16] What agreement [can there be between] a temple of God and idols? For we are the temple of the living God; even as God said, I will dwell in and with and among them and will walk in and with and among them, and I will be their God, and they shall be My people.

In the working of the world's ways humanity is the idols of its iniquity seen in the fact it is men and women who seek to be exalted by its social anarchy and ideals of self-alliance, especially where evil is at work in it. Though there is a devil behind all the wickedness and evil in the world, humanity's choice of such things to exalt oneself above others shows where it truly lies.

Believers on the other hand are to be of a statute that invokes a habitation of the Spirit of God that comes not by mediocrity of fellowship, but by a life that is from a transformed *spirit* and *soul*.

[17] So, come out from among [unbelievers], and separate (sever) yourselves from them, says the Lord, and touch not [any] unclean thing; then I will receive you kindly and treat you with favor, [18] And I will be a Father to you, and you shall be My sons and daughters, says the Lord Almighty.

A term widely used today is *social behavior* and in reference to the study of *physiology* and *sociology*, or in the most basics of it, one's behavioral activity directed towards other person or persons. Within society today there is a discontentment over all things not being as a few would have us believe they need to be. And of course, *society* being typically a group of people commonly related to each other, reveals many of the ideals or ideologies put forth are now becoming foundational platforms for the churches.

Thus, the social behavior among believers, is to reveal spiritual transformation that is by relationship with Christ and all members of the family of God. It is not based on the fact faith in Him includes a relationship with the Father God, and the Holy Spirit.

However, before I go too far, there is an issue that needs to be discussed in the Church concerning the very nature of those who are coming into fellowship of late and taking habitation among those in right standing in Christ.

Transformed – Spiritually.

Psalm 94:12-23 *[12] Blessed is the man whom thou chastenest, O LORD, and teachest him out of thy law; [13] That thou mayest give him rest from the days of adversity, until the pit be digged for the wicked. [14] For <u>the LORD will not cast off his people</u>, neither will <u>he forsake his inheritance</u>. [15] But <u>judgment shall return unto righteousness</u>: and <u>all the upright in heart shall follow it</u>.*

This is about churches having leadership unwilling to face the fact they by a pandering mannerism are inviting those who are not coming in to become a believer but by a covert spirit disrupt the flow of the Spirit of God. They are focused on changing the spiritual flow at the pulpit and amidst the congregation, they do well in exercising good works but are not changed by any transformational truths for *spirit* and *soul*.

I am not talking about driving out any hopeful converts I am talking about protecting the spiritual wellbeing of every sibling in Christ. The latest warfare tactic of our enemy is where people are attending churches under auspices of pandered ministerial acts by leadership coming in intent on changing the faith of those attending.

These are individuals not hanging on the promises of God, or the mercy of the Lord, they hang on the social activism of the day and equate fellowship by a gangland mentality that is relevant to an evil mannerism.

[16] <u>Who will rise up for me against the evildoers</u>? or <u>who will stand up for me against the workers of iniquity</u>? [17] Unless the LORD had been my help, my soul had almost dwelt in silence. [18] When I said, My foot slippeth; thy mercy, O LORD, held me up.

Many church leaders have already turned congregants over to these bands of socialist forces who see church as the last bastion for anti-liberal and white supremacist rhetoric. These same leaders, now spend time not in preparation for pulpit dissertations of Christ but political subjugation.

¹⁹ In the multitude of my thoughts within me thy comforts delight my soul. ²⁰ Shall the throne of iniquity have fellowship with thee, which frameth mischief by a law? ²¹ <u>They gather themselves together against the soul of the righteous,</u> and <u>condemn the innocent blood.</u>

One more reason, spiritual mediocrity is on the rise as many of the believers in these churches have given up on seeing a return to the days of signs, wonders, and miracles common among churches and ministries of the past.

These workers of iniquity and that what I choose to call them, see themselves fully justified in what they do emboldened by the lawlessness that prevails on our streets and in our government. They have no real spiritual consciousness of the things of God and see the activity of the Spirit of God and the word as contributors to a supremacy in humanity.

But take heart the creator of all is not going to let Christ prize possession be skewed to a point of being spiritually unrecognizable. He by authority of His word and the Spirit will continue to bring about matured offspring in this day of iniquity and they will be the workers of righteousness assisting in the cleansing of His Church in its last days.

²² But <u>the LORD is my defence;</u> and <u>my God is the rock of my refuge</u>. ²³ And <u>he shall bring upon them their own iniquity, and shall cut them off in their own wickedness;</u> yea, the LORD our God shall cut them off.

Let us get back to the subject at hand, there are Christians today who see themselves as part of a ministering body, but not as a sibling of God's spiritual family this helps create a spiritual independence to the matters of the body of Christ and eliminates any unity of love among the fellowship by the Holy Spirit.

The fact we are a part of a body of believers in Christ should be understood in the aspects of any transformation He says must take place. Paul explains in the following verse the grace of God being in us is what brings a mutual agreement regarding giving to his work in ministry.

2 Cor 9:14 ^(AMP) *And <u>they yearn for you while they pray for you</u>, because of the surpassing measure of God's grace (His favor and mercy and spiritual blessing which is shown forth) in you.*

Because of grace we must have mutual love for one another, not as casual acquaintances, but as ***affectionate spiritual siblings***, who desire a presence and character of our Father be in each of us. As in a natural family all members are deeply socially familiar with each other, and even though they may not all think and act alike they are comfortable with each other's presence. Because they have spent time together nurturing a love for one another due to the bond they have through heritage and lineage.

Now I know in the natural every family is not perfect, and some come from broken families, but for sake of understanding let us consider this to be what happens when things are right. Unity of the family of God is not built upon the same foundation as families in the natural, instead is built upon a spiritual perspective founded on the truth of God's word. Each sibling must be able to accept others governed by agape love expressed toward them.

Transformed to Love.

Phil 1:8-10 ^(NKJV) *For God is my witness, <u>how greatly I long for you all with the affection of Jesus Christ</u>.*

The affection expressed here is ***AGAPE***, the God kind of love that is to abound more and more, even to the full extent of perfect development. This is not the typical affectionate and emotional love we call *PHILEO* that occurs by a social activity.

But the kind of love that comes from being an active family by the Spirit of God. As I said, relationship with unbelievers provides no spiritual atmosphere capable of transformation and/or perfection of AGAPE in a believer. You can express agape toward them, but unless they receive Christ, they will not understand the true purpose of it.

⁹ And this I pray, <u>that your love may abound still more and more in knowledge and all discernment</u>, ¹⁰ that you may approve the things that are excellent, that you may be sincere and without offense till the day of Christ, ¹¹ being filled with the fruits of righteousness which are by Jesus Christ, to the glory and praise of God.

Now, here are some more things many of you may not like as it reflects poorly on our ability to love as the word says we should, but it is necessary to make this known so we can grow beyond these immature actions and be who God says we are.

1 Cor 13:3-10 *(BBE) 3 And if <u>I give all my goods to the poor</u>, and if I <u>give my body to be burned</u>, but <u>have not love</u>, it is of no profit to me.*

How many of you were taught that sacrifice is a way of life for a believer, and you must be willing to die for a witness or testimony of Jesus, and give up all possessions as loss in result of ministry to show His love. A religious application of truths regarding sacrifice for Christ's sake, but the reason I make such a statement is because it is not done based on revealing Agape love, but a love of self, such sacrificial manners only help to rectify any faults one may have.

As mentioned before for centuries leadership has had the idea sheep are expendable assets for work of ministry some even see them as helpless members of a flock to be slaughtered over and over by tithing and spiritual burn out through religious works.

Transformed – Spiritually.

⁴ Love is never tired of waiting; love is kind; love has no envy; love has no high opinion of itself, love has no pride; ⁵ Love's ways are ever fair, it takes no thought for itself; it is not quickly made angry, <u>it takes no account of evil</u>;

Agape is a supernatural love founded upon spiritual principles woven throughout the very character of God. Thus, based on truths of what is said here and in other areas of the word there is no way one could deem others as non-essential to the cause of Christ, to do so reflects Agape is not being exercised toward all God's offspring.

⁶ It takes no pleasure in wrongdoing, but has joy in what is true; ⁷ Love has the power of undergoing all things, having faith in all things, hoping all things. ⁸ Though the prophet's word may come to an end, tongues come to nothing, and knowledge have no more value, <u>love has no end</u>.

This love we call Agape is eternal in its working as it is the very nature of God who also has no end. If we add to this the fact anyone in Christ is an eternal essence, then Agape is to reflect exactly what the word says.

⁹ For our knowledge is only in part, and the prophet's word gives only a part of what is true: ¹⁰ But when that which is complete is come, then that which is in part will be no longer necessary.

While we know by scripture God does not see us as perfect there is one thing in scripture that we can become perfect at, it is in Agape the very love of God received as part of our transformation.

1 John 4:7-13 *⁷ Beloved, let us love one another: for love is of God; and everyone that loveth is born of God, and knoweth God.*

If no one's sacrifice except that of Jesus Christ the Son of God can change one's sinful status in the sight of God, then why sacrifice others in His name? I said, I would say things you would not like, but it is to bring to your perception that Agape is His love.

Which is not built upon any sacrifices we offer but on one sacrifice, Jesus's life given for all.

⁸ He that loveth not knoweth not God; for God is love. ⁹ In this was manifested the love of God toward us, because that God sent his only begotten Son into the world, that we might live through him.

Spiritually mediocre children are often sacrificed by leadership for sake of ministry so that the dynamics of the works being done are never seen as ineffective. This is affirmed in the fact ministries today no longer see benefit in bible study groups or home cells or even small group gatherings. And many no longer provide a subject specific teaching on anything from the scriptures.

¹⁰ Herein is love, not that we loved God, but that he loved us, and sent his Son to be the propitiation for our sins. ¹¹ Beloved, if God so loved us, we ought also to love one another. ¹² No man hath seen God at any time. If we love one another, God dwelleth in us, and his love is perfected in us. ¹³ Hereby know we that we dwell in him, and he in us, because he hath given us of his Spirit.

Our learning this truth takes us toward a perfection in Agape that is only seen through eyes that see us as the father sees us. Love in the perspective of God's nature is not love that sees others as just ministerial assets or liabilities but as equal in value by Agape for all the creation of humanity.

Math 5:43-48 *⁴³ Ye have heard that it hath been said, Thou shalt love thy neighbour, and hate thine enemy. ⁴⁴ But I say unto you, Love your enemies, bless them that curse you, do good to them that hate you, and pray for them which despitefully use you, and persecute you;*

Until the day we will see all things clearly as God we are to be transformed to be as He is in nature loving as He loves.

Transformed – Spiritually.

⁴⁵ That <u>ye may be the children of your Father which is in heaven</u>: for he maketh his sun to rise on the evil and on the good, and sendeth rain on the just and on the unjust. ⁴⁶ For if ye love them which love you, what reward have ye? do not even the publicans the same? ⁴⁷ And if ye salute your brethren only, what do ye more than others? do not even the publicans so? ⁴⁸ <u>Be ye therefore perfect</u>, <u>even as your Father which is in heaven is perfect</u>.

CHAPTER TEN
Ready for Harvest

Gen 17:7 And I will establish My covenant between Me and you and your descendants after you in their generations, for an everlasting covenant, to be God to you and your descendants after you.

The redemptive work of Christ, though not yet fulfilled in his time was accounted to Abraham because he believed in God, as previously said. Everything pertaining to relationship with Him is fully based on Christ birth, life, death, resurrection, and ascension. And evident that relationship with God is established upon covenant based upon principles that were fulfilled by Christ.

Heb 12:23-24 To the <u>general assembly and church of the firstborn</u>, <u>which are written in heaven</u>, and to God the Judge of all, and to the spirits of just men made perfect, ²⁴ And to <u>Jesus the mediator of the new covenant</u>, and <u>to the blood</u> of sprinkling, <u>that speaketh better things than that of Abel</u>.

All who become part of the Church age are brought into a new covenant through Christ and anyone in the covenant is expected to associate and interact in a manner based on its righteous principles.

The word righteousness in the Old Testament is privy to many extensive studies for a real meaning of it in Hebrew culture resulting in varied study elements pertaining to its structure. But it is the _noun_ composition of it that reveals interesting facts are associated. Here it is the Hebrew word (**_sedāqâ_**) which carries in it a sense of *loyalty, truthfulness, a demonstration of mercy, and/or to judge righteously, faithful to fulfill expectations and demonstrate one's honor.*

All of this has an underlying legality or manner of justice to be conformed to, in other words if one is righteous then they by a legal process or term are accepted as standing rightly with the one who is the most righteous judge of them.

Ps 50:5-6 *(AMP)* *Gather together to Me My saints [those who have found grace in My sight], those who have made a covenant with Me by sacrifice.* [6] *And the heavens declare His righteousness (rightness and justice), for God, He is judge. Selah [pause, and calmly think of that]!*

Any judgments God faithfully makes in respect to creation, will be done in a manner that corresponds to righteousness and justice since it is inherently within His nature to do so, as revealed by the Holy Spirit.

Ps 96:13 *Before the LORD: for he cometh, for he cometh to judge the earth: he shall judge the world with righteousness, and the people with his truth.*

In the Greek, the word (**_dikaiosynē_**) is translated righteousness meaning *"to reveal the character or quality of being right or just"* this word helps to bring the meaning of righteousness more into focus for understanding. We could say what is revealed to us about righteousness are the very statutes of God's established nature and essence seen as the one who faithfully occupies the most eternally right position.

Furthermore, in having such a position underlies any judgment to be applied to every manner of one's past life secured by faith in Jesus Christ resulting in right standing with the one who judges. It is God's love for humanity as to why He has provided a way for all who believe in His Son to have a right to a personal relationship with Him.

The behavior of the world is not one of right standing with God this is evident all over the place, and it is why it is important now more than ever before that God's children manifest a life, He would call righteous.

John 1:12-13 *But as many as received him, <u>to them gave he the right to become children of God</u>, even to them that believe on his name:* ¹³ *who were born, not of blood, nor of the will of the flesh, nor of the will of man, but of God.*

Jesus came so that anyone who believes in Him as the Son of God would be made righteous, and have access to interaction with the very God who created them. In a sense Christ sacrifice connected the creator to His creation by restoring a relationship God purposed from the beginning

2 Cor 5:17-18 ^(GW) *Whoever is a believer in Christ is a new creation. The old way of living has disappeared. A new way of living has come into existence.* ¹⁸ *God has done all this. <u>He has restored our relationship with him through Christ</u>, and has given us this ministry of restoring relationships.*

All believers need to know they are to have a *new way of living* while reconciling others to God through Christ, by the Holy Spirit. And that there is a spiritual purpose for a believer to live righteously, as it keeps before them the truth of who they are so that they emanate an image of God in their life.

However, many believers do not know they can be of the same nature as the Father and the Son, resulting in failure to reveal a manner of relationship that is to be spiritually occurring. There is a spirit of despair that continuously runs through churches constantly promoting judgments and discords. Mannerisms such as these prevent righteously founded behavior so when it comes to God and His relationship to us, we need to think of it this way.

If God were to reveal himself in your presence what would be the manner of His *behavior,* He actively directs toward you? In other words how is going to act? Well, by what is revealed in scripture it would reveal His-*loyalty, truthfulness, mercy,* and *righteousness judgment that is just,* seen a nature *faithful to fulfill* all expectations expressed through *love.*

God is much more than this, but these are some of His revealed characteristics, of His nature and essence as a righteous God. Jesus ensured anyone believing in Him would be established in a legally justified manner that is acceptable in a covenant established by His shed blood founded upon right standing with the Father. All of this is for a purposed process of interacting corporally with us, and as a result everyone in Christ has a behavior that is rightly mannered, as God is toward them.

In the old days they had Church socials where all would gather to meet with one another, and eat and act like everyone got along great. Most of the people there did not truly know one another, at least in a spiritual sense, they just socialized in a worldly manner as among everyone else they knew.

The problem was they were trying to bring spiritual unity by a fellowship contrary to truth as revealed in the word. If we look at how Jesus behaved here on earth, we see He lived to reveal the Father through a righteous way of life.

He told his disciples His interaction with His Father is revealed through His behavior which was a visible result of His own right standing.

John 14:6-11 *(GW) Jesus answered him, "I am the way, the truth, and the life. <u>No one goes to the Father except through me</u>. ⁷ If you have known me, you will also know my Father. From now on you know him {through me} and have seen him {in me}." ⁸ Philip said to Jesus, "Lord, show us the Father, and that will satisfy us."*

He goes on to tell them to believe that it is the Father doing all things through Him, but if you cannot believe that the Father is in Me, then believe by what you see Me doing.

⁹ Jesus replied, "I have been with all of you for a long time. Don't you know me yet, Philip? <u>The person who has seen me has seen the Father</u>. So how can you say, 'Show us the Father'? ¹⁰ Don't you believe that I am in the Father and the Father is in me? What I'm telling you doesn't come from me. The Father, who lives in me, does what he wants. <u>Believe me when I say that I am in the Father and that the Father is in me</u>. Otherwise, <u>believe me because of the things I do</u>.

We can break this down to a simple explanation, that says there is a correctly acceptable manner of fellowship, or social interaction, God expects to occur among those born into the family of God. A social interaction established by a covenant that reveals a righteous statute is applied. So, the very nature and essence of God is to be manifested by those now in covenant to Him by the Holy Spirit.

Something you may not know, all believers are under God's theocratic authority to eternally dominate cultural expectations common to regions represented, in this case, it is the kingdom of God. <u>Did you get that?</u> God who created all things presents himself, righteously, so perceptively it means everyone in relationship with Him must be able to interact having this same standing.

Thus, a question appears that ask; Is a believer made righteous or do they have to earn such a status by presenting a certain kind of behavior? God makes no requirement of humanity to become righteous on its own and He explains that any effort of our own righteousness we might exert is to Him seen as filthy rags. Which in translation, is an actual reference to a woman's menstrual garments, so I think you can get a picture of why right standing in Christ is a paramount issue in a relationship with God.

Isa 64:6 *6 But we are all as an unclean thing, and <u>all our righteousnesses are as filthy rags</u>; and we all do fade as a leaf; and our iniquities, like the wind, have taken us away.*

Rightness with God is not something we can earn, or a position ordained upon certain individuals. It is an applied state of being that comes upon everyone who by faith receives Jesus Christ as Lord and Savior, and is a result of His sacrifice.

2 Co 5:20 *20 Now then we are ambassadors for Christ, as though God did beseech you by us: we pray you in Christ's stead, be ye reconciled to God. 21 For he hath made him to be sin for us, who knew no sin; that <u>we might be made the righteousness of God in him</u>.*

I know you are saying I am not God or Christ so how can I reveal such a manner of life! It is only by the Holy Spirit that anyone can truly reveal such a lifestyle in the world. Therefore, willingness to be led by the Spirit of God is paramount to being able to do it as the Father has expectation of it occurring.

Rom 8:14 *For as many as are led by the Spirit of God, <u>they are the sons of God</u>.*

Look at this statement from Jesus again - *Believe me when I say that I am in the Father and that the Father is in me. Otherwise, believe me because of the things I do.* He said if you cannot believe what I say is true then believe by what you see me do.

Though all are made righteous in Christ by what He suffered and died for, God saw fit to afford such a status to Noah and others in the Old Testament because of faith in Him. This relationship between God and those who believe did not start at the cross, but was purposed long before Christ hung on it. Jesus is at the core of all things that pertain to yours and my righteous status.

Since our sinful life before Jesus saved us was situated in the curse and accounted as unrighteous, our life is now situated in Christ righteousness. Therefore, the preceding paragraphs reveal how believers are to live in such a way it manifests their right standing with God through Jesus Christ. Fulfilling by witness and testimony of not only who He is but who they are, as sons and daughters of God.

Any spiritual mediocrity present in and among those who are to be righteous promotes a wrong witness and testifies of something other than the truth of who they are made to be in Him. The following scripture reveals one has inheritance by faith in Jesus and therefore not only shares His suffering but His glory.

Rom 8:17 *(AMP) And if we are [His] children, then we are [His] heirs also: <u>heirs of God and fellow heirs with Christ</u> [sharing His inheritance with Him]; only <u>we must share His suffering if we are to share His glory</u>.*

The Greek word translated heir in this verse is (**_klēronomos_**) meaning to *"possess or obtain <u>a lot</u> or <u>portion</u> of something"* in this case an inheritance that is jointly shared with Jesus Christ, the Son of God. This is provisionally available to all who are called offspring of the Highest since they are in right standing by Christ Jesus.

In ministry the focus is to get people to see they are a sinner in need of a savior and for the most part this is true but in the process of this presentation they must know why they are counted as sinners before God.

This issue must be made apparent to them, as it is a fact, they are not in right standing with the God of all creation because His righteous character is not in acceptance of sin. The age-old aspect of revealing righteousness as it pertains to Christ and His work is no longer the main theme in many churches of today, instead it is to pander to people's sins hopeful they will see a need for a life, better than the one they now live.

This leads to exactly what I have been talking about, spiritual mediocrity among the saints who are struggling to live in a righteous manner according to the Spirit of God. There is a constant witness of this today in society where we have those who call themselves Christians but speak using cursive words the same as unbelievers making them appear the same in character. And watch the same media content and act in a manner that says they are no different.

Thankfully, God is faithful to fulfill all His prophetic promises to those who are of an inheritance with Christ. And He has proposed for His spiritual lineage to be just as He says they are in His sight having a right to be called His offspring. Since no one who believes in Christ is greater than another, as such there is no son or daughter who has an inheritance greater than any others.

Through Christ all are made righteous and equally positioned as heirs to the promises of God having possession of all blessings to be distributed on this earth while exercising a spiritual dominion that He decreed to be in appearance upon it.

Gen 1:28 And God blessed them, and God said unto them, Be fruitful, and multiply, and replenish the earth, and subdue it: and have dominion *over the fish of the sea, and over the fowl of the air, and over every living thing that moveth upon the earth.*

We have already seen that a transfer of supernatural blessings in the spiritual realm into this earth is only possible through His heirs of righteousness.

God's sons, and daughters who by right standing in Christ are situated to be blessed to bless others and inherit it all according to the promise.

Ps 37:22 *(AMP)* *For such as are blessed of God shall [in the end] inherit the earth, but they that are cursed of Him shall be cut off.*

In the whole of the history of God's creation there will never be another time like the Church Age, we are the only ones here for such a time as this.

Therefore, our having ability to fulfill our part in God's plan for this age as believers, requires certain things be in manifestation that reveal His very nature and essence on this earth is through grace, a key principle of Christ righteousness.

John 1:16-17 *And of his fullness have all we received, and grace for grace.* *17* *For the law was given by Moses, but grace and truth came by Jesus Christ.*

Believers revealing Christ to this world is all done under God's grace, which is a measure of His favor that is afforded through Christ Jesus. And favor that is unearned, and cannot be merited by anything they do, but only by what His Son has done. Grace is something He places upon all who believe in Christ, who are also to have grace upon others.

The fact sin and iniquity still abound among humanity is more reason grace is needed, but today grace abounding toward others is heavily ladened with religious deeds and self-imposed efforts for ministerial rights. Making a witness and testimony as a believer in Christ difficult for revealing the character, or nature and essence of God.

Those who are lost are the *objective of grace*, not a source or means of it, since grace for them should be what promotes in us the desire to reveal the Father's love through Christ Jesus our Lord.

All believers must listen carefully to what the Holy Spirit is saying to them both inwardly and by the scriptures, as His witness is for their perfection in God's grace and love.

1 John 4:4-13 *(NKJV) You are of God, little children, and have overcome them, because He who is in you is greater than he who is in the world. ⁵ They are of the world. Therefore, they speak as of the world, and the world hears them. ⁶ We are of God. He who knows God hears us; he who is not of God does not hear us. <u>By this we know the spirit of truth and the spirit of error</u>.*

God is not fooling around here; it was and still is important for Him to reveal these truths by the Spirit and the word. Grace does not mean we are to accept the sins of others, but it does mean we need to accept the fact they like us need a savior from sin. And that we can reveal grace toward them while we are helping them to know Christ and come to receive Him as Lord and savior.

I fully believe grace and love are key principles of righteousness and if they are revealed in what we do then the Spirit of God has liberty to move in supernatural ways. This affirms an image through us that aligns to His will being done.

⁷ Beloved, <u>let us love one another, for love is of God</u>; and everyone who loves is born of God and knows God. ⁸ He who does not love does not know God, for God is love. ⁹ In this the love of God was manifested toward us, that God has sent His only begotten Son into the world, that we might live through Him.

Many churches today offer a miss-skewed manner of His love expressed and coming forth from pulpits and many other areas of the Church. It is miss-skewed because of what many are calling love, is not true Agape love but affectionate desires to fulfill emotional exergies brought on by anxiousness egos fulfilling a so-called loving and caring mannerism as they are taught by pulpits.

¹⁰ In this is love, not that we loved God, but that <u>He loved us and sent His Son to be the propitiation for our sins</u>.

The kind of love as John reveals here is the light of Agape the love that God is. But a lust for things like financial stability, peer acceptance, and all kinds of social entanglements removes this love and replaces it with a "love" that is more in line to emotional lust.

¹¹ Beloved, <u>if God so loved us</u>, <u>we also ought to love one another</u>. ¹² No one has seen God at any time. <u>If we love one another, God abides in us</u>, and <u>His love has been perfected in us</u>. ¹³ By this we know that we abide in Him, and He in us, because He has given us of His Spirit.

Another key principle for the body of Christ to know is by an influence of the Spirit of God, a promotion of love for one another will not allow those mediocrely perfected in some other kind of love to hold positions of authority in their heart.

Look at **verse 12** God abides in us this alone sets the standard for what manner of life is to be in interaction here based on His love being brought to fruition. If believers love one another He abides in the love, this principle is written to those who are in Christ, and refers to how the love that He is, is to be perfected in every believer so a nature within has His love for one another.

Let us also look back at **Verse 11** where it says, if God loved us then we ought to love one another. This whole principle is for the believer, and is all about loving other believers, and developing an Agape love, so all will reveal such a love to those in darkness, or who we call unbelievers.

Since grace which means unearned favor with God comes by loving as He loves, as sons and daughters we must have grace or the same kind of favor toward each other.

However, many today are too eager to abstain from fellowship regarding another spiritual sibling simply because they made a mistake, or they are not in line to their way of thinking socially. Every time this happens there is no real understanding of grace revealed, thus an uncharacteristic love appears serving to promote immaturity regarding truth that reveals His grace for all.

I am every believer's spiritual brother, and I know I need the Agape love of God from every one of you, my brothers, and sisters, to help me nurture God's love in me by the Holy Spirit. Any believer can take refuge in their relationship with Christ and be nurtured by the love of God without anyone else, but to live in this manner is out of character to Agape fulfilling a commandment of loving yourself.

Luke 10:27 ²⁷ *And he answering said, Thou shalt love the Lord thy God with all thy heart, and with all thy soul, and with all thy strength, and with all thy mind; and thy neighbour as thyself.*

The spiritual wellbeing of the Church, as the body of Christ, is dependent upon a corporate sibling healthiness, which is nurtured by righteous interactions with other siblings as led by the Holy Spirit founded on truths of the word. And since no one separates God from the love that He is, it reveals that such a love must be in everything a believer does. Add to this the fact that no one can separate the Holy Spirit from Agape means it is the only love that changes others.

Heb 10:24-25 ^(GW) *We must also consider how to encourage each other to show love and to do good things. *²⁵* We should not stop gathering together with other believers, as some of you are doing. Instead, we must continue to encourage each other even more as we see the day of the Lord coming.*

Take note of *verse 25,* the writer says *believers* must encourage each other, this is accomplished only by all members of Christ body not just those gifted in ministry at the pulpits.

Though they are the ones called to instruct and edify activity to be manifested by all parts of the body, as to be seen by those in the world. It is important in these last hours of the Church's ministry that those who will be a part of an end time harvest are the workers Christ said the fields are ripe for harvest of. But mediocre workers will not only have difficulty revealing the grace and love of God to those who are lost but the power to bring change.

There is No Gospel of Mediocrity

What we have seen is for the Holy Spirit to bring forth any supernatural signs, wonders, and miracles confirming a witness and testimony of righteousness in Christ, it is necessary we as children of God be the revealers of it.

Mark 16:20 [20] And they went forth, and preached everywhere, the Lord working with them, and <u>confirming the word with signs following</u>. Amen.

However, reality is most believers fail miserably in attempting to reveal righteousness to the world. Therefore, God is not counting on us to be the perfect witness, it is the glory of the Lord by the work of the Spirit through us that draws people to Christ. And He will never fail to reveal the righteous character of the Father in doing so.

John 12:32 [32] And I, if I be lifted up from the earth, will draw all men unto me.

Since it is the Spirit of God who draws people to Christ in doing the work of the Father on earth. The facts are He by an inner witness brings conviction of one's need to be in right standing with God, so a judgment of sin is no longer upon them. This means a believer's right standing in Christ cannot by uncharacteristic mediocrity reveal Christ righteousness.

John 6:44 [44] No man can come to me, <u>except the Father which hath sent me draw him</u>: and I will raise him up at the last day.

The bible is filled with all truths pertaining to everything God ordained and promised for humanity during this 7000-year event on earth, and our part in this is written in and among all of it for His glory. Nothing is said about His word not being able to do as He has spoken, but in every aspect, it clearly proves to be true and faithful to fulfill exactly what it says.

Thus, you have seen God's power is in His word to accomplish His will, therefore the two most important aspects of this are the Holy Spirit and the word, both effective in transforming anyone into who He says they are to be in Christ Jesus. Spiritual mediocrity is not a result of anything the Holy Spirit has or has not done by the word of God, but is a result of issues that are occurring throughout the world and in the Church affecting the spiritual lives of believers for a purpose of removing any consciousness of who they are.

In case you did not know every believer is held responsible for their personal growth and maturity in the things of God, and it is not done to punish if you fail to line up to some outlined truth for spiritual wellbeing. But to hold you accountable for becoming what He says you are to be. This reveals a personal relationship with the Father upheld by faith able to commune by the Spirit over what and where spiritual blessings are to operate is ultimate righteousness believers can offer aside from the life of His first-born Son.

Heb 1:5-9 5 For unto which of the angels said he at any time, Thou art my Son, this day have I begotten thee? And again, I will be to him a Father, and he shall be to me a Son? ⁶ And again, when he bringeth in the firstbegotten into the world, he saith, And let all the angels of God worship him. ⁷ And of the angels he saith, Who maketh his angels spirits, and his ministers a flame of fire. ⁸ But unto the Son he saith, Thy throne, O God, is for ever and ever: a sceptre of righteousness is the sceptre of thy kingdom. ⁹ Thou hast loved righteousness, and hated iniquity; therefore God, even thy God, hath anointed thee with the oil of gladness above thy fellows.

This makes where you attend church as important as the union you have in Christ with the Father. Since it is to be the place where you, by spiritual sense, plug into a fellowship with others who are all influenced by the same truths as the Holy Spirit reveals them from the word.

To avoid spiritual mediocrity, one must simply do according to what is written in scripture believing that the power within is fully able to do what it says. Your faith acting upon truth is all that is needed. I know this seems more easily said than done, but it is as simple as you having faith in the one who brought salvation to you, Jesus the Son of God.

Though we have seen throughout this book the real enemy is the devil; he is the one who is out to discourage you or even destroy your faith if possible. However, the Spirit of God and the power of the word are more than enough to sustain you with a vigilance that he cannot take away.

As a believer you must avoid anyone who caters to the ways of this world, as it only diminishes your faith. This applies to both lay and minister alike since it is not in the annals of scripture for one to be a sufferer of ignorance and/or abused in some manner for the sake of another's mediocrity.

Jesus had John write the book of revelation to be understood by all who have faith to receive truth within it. This is so those who are holding on to it will be able to withstand the days of iniquity coming upon the earth before His return.

Rev 1:3-6 3 *Blessed is he that readeth, and they that hear the words of this prophecy, and keep those things which are written therein: for the time is at hand. ⁴ John to the seven churches which are in Asia: Grace be unto you, and peace, from him which is, and which was, and which is to come; and from the seven Spirits which are before his throne;*

If we see truth as the Spirit reveals, then what is said in the following verses is the culmination of the intent and concern in our Father's heart for all who become His. It is the character of spiritual mediocrity that encourages believers to find no harbor in such truth for a life in Christ both now and to come.

⁵ And from Jesus Christ, who is the faithful witness, and the first begotten of the dead, and the prince of the kings of the earth. Unto him that loved us, and washed us from our sins in his own blood, ⁶ And hath made us kings and priests unto God and his Father; to him be glory and dominion for ever and ever. Amen.

1. **Religion in A Handbasket**
   Israel, The Church, and The Pulpit
2. **The Power of God Revealed**
   In the Authority of His Word
3. **From Rib to Righteousness Marriage Series Book 1**
   Is Marriage an Extinct Union or Eternal Instincts?
4. **What from Hell is Going on In the Church?**
5. **From Rib to Righteousness Marriage Series Book 2**
   The Three P's of Marriage
6. **Basically Evil**
   Is the Devil Evil by Nature? Is Humanity Evil by Choice?
   Having sense enough to answer these questions can make
   the difference between Life and Death.

All books are available in paperback and e-reader formats.
at all major bookstores and e-commerce outlets.

Made in the USA
Columbia, SC
26 June 2021